D1131108

THE MAN WITH KALEIDOSCOPE EYES

ALSO BY TIM LUCAS

FICTION

Throat Sprockets (1994)
The Book of Renfield: A Gospel of Dracula (2005)
The Secret Life of Love Songs (2019)
The Man with Kaleidoscope Eyes (2022)
The Only Criminal (forthcoming)

NON-FICTION

Your Movie Guide to Movie Classics Video Tapes & Discs (1985)
Your Movie Guide to Horror Video Tapes & Discs (1985)
Your Movie Guide to Science Fiction Video Tapes & Discs (1985)
Your Movie Guide to Mystery / Suspense Video Tapes & Discs (1985)
The Video Watchdog Book (1992)
Mario Bava—All the Colors of the Dark (2007)
Studies in the Horror Film: Videodrome (2008)
Midnight Movie Monographs:
Spirits of the Dead / Histoires Extraordinaires (2018)
Midnight Movie Monographs:
Succubus / Necronomicon (forthcoming)

THE MAN WITH KALEIDOSCOPE EYES

TIM LUCAS

Based on the Original Screenplay by
Tim Lucas & Charlie Largent
with Michael Almereyda & James Robison

THE MAN WITH KALEIDOSCOPE EYES

COVER ART

Published in May 2022 by Electric Dreamhouse, an imprint of
PS Publishing Ltd. by arrangement with the author.

FIRST EDITION

ISBNs
978-1-78636-839-3
978-1-78636-840-9 [signed edition]

Design & Layout by Michael Smith
Printed and bound in England by T.J. Books

PS PUBLISHING
Grosvenor House
1 New Road
Hornsea, HU18 1PG
England

editor@pspublishing.co.uk
www.pspublishing.co.uk

ACKNOWLEDGEMENTS

I WOULD LIKE TO THANK **Roger Corman**, **Julie Corman** and **Frances Doel**, all of whom were encouraging of this project and generous with their time and reminiscences; **Joe Dante** and **Elizabeth Stanley**, for believing in this project since Day One; my fellow screenwriters **Charlie Largent**, **Michael Almereyda**, and **James Robison**, each of whom contributed something special to this story's humor, tone, and overall make-up; my agent **Judy Coppage** for her years of advice, diligence, patience and tolerance; **Neil Snowdon** and **Pete & Nicky Crowther** for providing this book with such a warm and loving home; and (as ever) **Donna Lucas**, my wife and most meticulous proofreader, who has walked beside me each and every day of this journey.

As the saying goes, "What a long, strange trip it's been."

T. L.

For Roger, the real one.
Artist. Problem-solver. And a gentleman.

You are about to be involved in a most unusual reading experience.

This novel deals with the hallucinogenic drug LSD and the man who dared to make the first dramatic motion picture about this controversial subject.

While the principal characters are based with affection on real people, and the story has been informed by published interviews and accounts, what follows is (make no mistake) a novel—a work of fiction.

Therefore, it should at all times be kept in mind by the reader that, while the main points of the story are indeed factual, what binds these points together is largely imaginary.

"Words have no power to impress the mind without the exquisite horror of their reality."

—Edgar Allan Poe

"You're only as young as the last time you changed your mind."

—Timothy Leary

CHAPTER 1

NOVEMBER 1966

SUSAN FONDA, *NÉE* BREWER, strolled out of the upstairs bathroom into the adjoining bedroom of her Beverly Hills home. Freshly showered, she was garbed in a lightweight paisley caftan as she wrapped a tangerine towel around her long, wet hair, turban-style.

Her husband Peter was—unusually—exactly as she had left him about 20 minutes earlier, exactly as he had been when she first entered their bedroom an hour or so prior. Shirtless and barefoot, he was stretched out on the bed, half-sitting, his back supported by luxuriant pillows, his expression completely absorbed. Not because he had taken mushrooms or any other sort of hallucinogen; there was a spent roach in the bedside ashtray, but hardly any ash.

No, he was deeply engrossed in a film script messengered to their door earlier that day.

Peter was a white-noise kind of guy. He was reading with the radio on—KHJ, "Boss Radio." It was just past the top of the hour and a brief news report was in progress: *Estimates of Viet Cong deaths run to 2,000 for the week, with new fronts breaking along the Laotian and Cambodian borders where Americans, as has been repeatedly emphasized, are serving in a non-combat and advisory role only.*

Click.

Susan thought Peter might object to her turning the radio off, but he was somewhere else entirely. She crept into bed beside him, curled up and watched him read the last few pages in curious silence, waiting to be noticed.

As Peter read the closing words of the script's last printed page, she saw his lips part, his jaw drop slack in awe and disbelief. He closed the bound manuscript with something like solemnity.

"I can't believe you finished it," she said, mildly impressed. "You never finish a script."

To her surprise, a tear formed and spilled helplessly from his eye. "Oh, Jesus," he managed, half-gasp, half-chuckle. "Jesus H. Christ."

"Baby, are you crying?"

Peter felt almost paralyzed by the emotions dropped on him, detonating within him from what he'd just read. Everything he thought he knew about the business in which he made his living, everything he thought he knew about the world, particularly the innate limitations available to artistic expression, had suddenly and irrevocably changed. He wiped his cheek dry.

"I guess I am," he smiled, a bit self-consciously, embarrassed to be seen.

"Peter, what's wrong?"

"Nothing. That's what's so groovy! It's like . . . now everything's alright. This script . . . is such a mind-fuck. It's so . . . freaking beautiful. You have no idea . . ."

"Then tell me," she said, curling up to him. "What's it called?"

"*The Trip*."

"Road picture?"

"No, Susie Bear. It's about a man who takes acid." Then he held up his hand, as though to call a halt to time itself. "No, it's really about . . . It's really about acid *itself*."

Susan couldn't help tensing up a bit. She wasn't really into the drug scene. When she first heard of *lysergic acid diethylamide*, it wasn't considered in the same light as grass or cocaine; it wasn't seen as recreational. Though perfectly legal, it was a controlled substance accessed by people for use in sessions under the close supervision of doctors of psychiatric medicine. Then it became a kind of recreational drug, which led to its being declared illegal—initially in Nevada and California state.

She had never taken LSD, as people were now calling it. She knew that

Peter had some experience of it; he had, in fact, taken it several times—initially in 1965, and more recently as a means of coping with the loss of his best friend, Stormy—Eugene "Stormy" McDonald III, that is—the heir to the Zenith Radio fortune, who had taken his own life with a shotgun almost two years earlier in 1965. Stormy's death, and the violence of it, had reopened ripples in time, linking it to the 1960 overdose of his beloved Bridget Hayward (for whom they had named their daughter) and his mother's own suicide when he was only 10 years old. All this explained why, when Peter met The Beatles and took acid with them, he told John Lennon "I know what it's like to be dead." John hadn't been ready to know that, and used Beatle clout to have him shown the door.

Susan hadn't felt any need to use the drug to explore herself, but she had seen at close hand how it had helped Peter. It had made him a less neurotic, more self-accepting man. He had become less armored at home among his loved ones, more confident and assured in business, someone who was substantially more than just Henry's son. He didn't always see this because, when he looked at his dad, he saw something of himself and also something of Americana.

I dig my father. I wish he could open his eyes and dig me.

Susan intuited that the best thing she could do was to be available to Peter, to inhabit this moment with him. So she pressed him once again, gently: "Tell me more."

"It's incredible. There's one scene that contains something like 500 individual shots. He describes every one, and they're all right, all lucid, all... kinda inevitable, you know? Here, let me find it."

Peter rifled eagerly through the Xeroxed pages, near-crazed with gratification.

"The pages aren't even numbered; it's all so stream of consciousness. Wait, here it is. Now dig this..."

As Susan listened attentively, Peter rattled off an incoherent sequence of images: funeral man in white makeup, bouncing acorns, a blue spinning pinwheel, birds feeding, horses galloping along the beach, Buddha, a buffalo head nickel, bouquet of flowers, three monsters, spilling jewels.

Guess you had to be there, thought Susan...

Then, alerted by an emotion she seldom heard in his voice, maybe only that first time he held their child, she looked up from the printed page to her husband's face and saw another tear forming, pulsing over the curvature of his eye. She watched as it bulged, glittered, and broke over his lashes to glide through the stubble on his cheek.

"Sounds like you might want to do this one," she said.

He looked at her like she'd just made the understatement of the century.

"Want to do it? Susie Bear, I *have* to do it. This isn't some bullshit part like *Tammy and the Schmuckface*. This is going to be the most important film ever made in North America. Maybe anywhere."

Just like that, she was convinced. She knew he wasn't joking.

He continued: "I can't believe that I—of all people—could be fortunate enough to be asked to star in this movie."

"Who wrote it?" she asked.

"Jesus." For half a second, Susan almost mistook his exclamation for his answer—but then Peter added, "I didn't even look!"

Peter turned the script over and looked at the cover page. It was stamped "Property of The Corman Company."

Fuck me, he thought. How they had ever lucked into this brilliance, he had no idea.

Then he saw the byline.

"Jack Nicholson."

"Jack Nicholson?" she exclaimed.

Peter frowned. The name rang a dim bell.

"Oh, you remember! We've met him," Susan said brightly.

"Where?"

"I don't remember, some opening or party. He's an actor. I didn't know he was a writer."

"If he's an actor, why can't I place him?"

"Maybe he hasn't made anything notable. Just Corman stuff, right?"

"Susie Bear, *I'm* doing Corman stuff."

"Yeah, but I think he's been doing it for 10 years. If he hasn't made it yet . . ."

"He was made for nobler things," Peter said. He slapped the face of the screenplay in his lap. "He needs to know."

With that pronouncement, he scooted to the foot of the bed and started putting on his socks and boots.

"Where are you going!?"

"I've got to tell him."

"You mean right now?"

"You don't understand, Susie Bear. A mind this sensitive . . . He could be despairing. I've got to find him and tell him."

"Do you know where to find him?"

Peter halted in his tracks. "No."

Susan slipped off the bed. "Let me make a few calls. I hear he's quite the ladies' man."

It only took one. Susan returned fairly quickly with the information Peter needed: "I called Luana. It seems they're old pals. He's going through a divorce, crashing over at Harry Dean Stanton's place."

She saw her husband standing before her, all 6' 2" of him fully outfitted and primed for night flight, looking much like the character he'd just played in Roger Corman's *The Wild Angels*—leather jacket, tinted aviator glasses, skinny black leather trousers with racing stripes, Cuban heels.

Peter Fonda. The rock star who needed no guitar.

"Love you, Susie Bear," he grinned, kissing her cheek. "Now if I can only find my keys."

Downstairs, a three-year-old girl sat cross-legged in front of a television console, watching an old black-and-white movie. Peter ambled down the flight of stairs behind her, the heels of his boots making a familiar tattoo on its cascade of Spanish tiles.

"Hey, Bridge? You seen Daddy's chopper keys?"

The child barely reacted.

"Did you check your pockets?" Susan called down from upstairs.

Sure enough: there they were. As he was about to head out the front door, Peter took notice of the movie his daughter was watching: John Ford's *My Darling Clementine*. He walked over and scrunched down next to her.

"Know who that is?" he asked, pointing at a man on the screen.

"You?"

Peter smiled philosophically, as though his daughter had seen through his face to a wish cherished somewhere deep behind it.

"Naw," he confessed. "That's Henry. That's Gramps."

As one Fonda grabbed his saddle and swung onto his horse, outside—under the stars, amid the sounds of tree frogs and distant traffic—another Fonda swung onto his Harley, jammed in its key, engaged the engine, and raised heavy metal thunder. Then he rolled down the driveway to claim the open road as his own.

CHAPTER 2

JUNE 1966

SUNSET BOULEVARD IS A SNAKE of winding asphalt that spans an impressive 21.75 miles, from Figueroa Street in downtown Los Angeles to Pacific Coast Highway in the Palisades. The "Sunset Strip" (as its mile-and-a-half stretch through West Hollywood is popularly known) has always been synonymous with where the action is and—perhaps more importantly—where it's *going* to be. The word "street" seems unworthy of such a phenomenological magnet but, taking its myriad stories into account, it is a street—one where many futures have been made. Where else can teenage hitchhikers stand, with their thumb out, get picked up, and sign major studio contracts before they set foot on the sidewalk again?

It is also where the action has always been, the home turf to all the great Hollywood supper clubs—Ciro's, the Mocambo, Dino's Lounge, the Trocadero and Moulin Rouge—not the mention that notorious *pied-à-terre* of Hollywood royalty, the Chateau Marmont Hotel.

In the 1940s and '50s, as the Brylcreemed and bouffanted habitués of all those swank martini clubs began to be lured across the desert by the greener felt of the gaming tables in freshly built Las Vegas, the Strip entered a period of decline. This made it available to change—extreme change—a premonition, if you will, of what was about to take hold of the motion picture business that built this city on the dust of fool's gold. It was around this time that the city's Baby Boomers first stepped up to the plate, demanding their inheritance. The local scene began to metamorphose in curious response to their desires.

In the early 1960s, as KRLA blasted the happy sounds of The Beach Boys and Jan & Dean, their lyrics name-checking all the local landmarks from Colorado Boulevard to Doheny Drive, the Strip embarked on its own advent into modern mythology. It became the epicenter of endless summer; a place for cruising, for flexing the wings that were the birthright of the native Angeleno, for driving with the top down and feeling as one with all the sun and flesh and fame that Los Angeles, California had to offer. It became the city's great equalizer, its demilitarized zone, its Via Veneto.

New worlds of diversion appeared—the Whisky a Go Go, where the best local and out-of-town bands played and sometimes recorded live; The Body Shop, where you could see bosomy Russ Meyer starlets twirl their tassels up close and in person; Jay Ward Productions, with its Bullwinkle Moose statue on permanent outdoor display; and Tower Records, where you could shop for new music alongside the same people who were recording it. As tartar began to build up on the Hollywood smile of this new decade, it was no longer just the Strip. It became a scene—a fluorescent, bubbling Petrie dish of advertising for sights, sounds and styles, stacked wall-to-wall with neon signs and billboards trumpeting all that which had yet to come; the new movies and albums, the clothes and TV shows that the rest of the country (indeed, the rest of the world) would be talking about in the months ahead, for the year to come. Contrary to its name, Sunset was actually where the sun *rose*—on the American dream.

Depending on where you lived and how long you had lived there, the Sunset Strip might seem akin to the trenches that are sometimes dug and filled with gasoline by property owners to discourage the influx of fire ants, because the Strip also divided the most important section of the city. Below the Strip were the hotels and the cheaper properties, those without views, the refashioned flop houses where tourists stayed and wannabes paid too much rent for the privilege of an address they didn't mind leaving with casting agents as their own. Above the Strip were the Hollywood hills, much too steep to be walked on foot, where were piled the lavish homes of most everyone who divided their time between fantasy and reality in the worlds of film and television.

Come the Summer of 1966, a similar dividing line began to arise between the Hollywood old guard and its burgeoning *avant-garde*: the young, the long-haired, the colorfully and flowerfully-dressed. Such folk were hooked on the siren songs being sent out into the night air from Whisky a Go Go, the Troubadour, Pandora's Box, the Galaxy, the Kaleidoscope, Sneaky Pete's, and all the rest. It wasn't just the new establishments, either. Even Ciro's—struggling to stay open with their diminishing clientele—reluctantly kissed their old dress code goodbye and booked The Byrds.

The old guard may have taken to spending their weekends in Vegas but this didn't mean they had no objection to the unwashed kids moving in and taking over their old stomping grounds. It was still *their* Strip, after all. It wasn't the same as it had been, back in the day when Gazzari's had been Sherry's Restaurant, the joint where gangster Mickey Cohen got whacked in 1948, so the police were asked to start taking an interest in the vagrant element. Hippies started getting hassled, a few dozen took beatings regardless of gender. Ten o'clock curfews were introduced to discourage the 24-hour costume parties that had started taking place up and down the main drag.

The city may have been in flux but one beautiful thing about it remained constant: the billboards decorating its twists and turns with advertisements for the latest bumper crop of homegrown product. To Roger Corman's eyes, they were a glimpse into the future; they were science fiction. After all, it was this product and this product only that prepared not only Los Angeles but the rest of the country—even the world—for what was going to become important to everyone very soon, what they needed to look forward to, and start thinking about.

Born Free.

The Endless Summer.

The Game is Over.

The Wild Angels.

And yes, Herb Alpert and the Tijuana Brass, exclusively on A&M Records and Tapes.

A bass drum's *bom bom bom bom bom bom bom*, rising brushwork on the snare, giving way to dawning horns—this was the sound that jump-started mornings of late for Roger Corman. It was the opening instrumental trifecta announcing Herb Alpert's "A Taste Of Honey" from his hit album *Whipped Cream & Other Delights* sounding better than ever in the recently introduced 8-track cartridge format.

Roger found this Easy Listening instrumental hit the perfect complement to his morning drive into work. It sounded enterprising, somewhat urgent, and seemed to herald the promise of an exciting new week as his Mercedes convertible zoomed along the sun-kissed streets of Hollywood. Notoriously cheap, fine cars were Roger's only real indulgence. That, and the pride he felt when one of those billboards lining the Strip happened to be his.

At 41 years of age, he had been in the motion picture business for about 10 years. Remarkably, he had already produced in excess of 60 feature films—45 of which he also directed. Such productivity might be expected to age a man, yet Roger still looked much as he did in publicity photos documenting his mid- to late-20s. He was boyishly handsome, with no easily discernible gray in his dark brown hair, and had the bearing and charisma of a well-groomed, well-modulated, well-educated man.

If he had any fault at all, it was—by his own admission—that he had never given much thought to apparel. He had stumbled onto (or rather, into) a semblance of personal style back in his days at Stanford, where he studied engineering: plain slacks, canvas shoes, a V-necked cardigan over a white or pale-blue, buttoned-down shirt—or even a T-shirt, if he was running late. On days when the sun was particularly aggressive, he might add a wilted-looking bucket hat and a pair of Foster Grants. The sunglasses sufficed for this particular mellow morning, coming up fast on 9:30.

The storefronts, stop lights, and billboards lining the Strip arced across Roger's lenses as he navigated the familiar route that took him from his West LA digs to his present office on the Columbia Studios lot at Gower and Sunset. It was one of those "only in Hollywood" stories: though broadly identified with the independent company American International Pictures—identified with Frankie and Annette's *Beach Party* pictures and his own Edgar Allan Poe series—he had signed a three-picture deal with the major and been given a three-room office on their studio lot; however, so far, he had been unsuccessful in engaging the company with any of his pitches. So, he was in effect accepting their hospitality while continuing to generate new product for AIP.

Roger pulled into his reserved parking space, just outside his office building where his personal assistant Frances Doel stood awaiting him. Frances was British and in her early 20s; she was tall and slender with fine red hair crowning a peaches-and-cream complexion. In the relatively short time since she had become a Californian, she had come to know all the right stores and, having a nose for sales, quickly mastered the art of presenting an attractive and fashionable look on a budget.

"You're scary, Roger!" she exclaimed with her appealing Oxford accent.

"I am?" Roger grinned, climbing out of his car. "Why?"

"Nine-thirty sharp every morning."

"Punctuality is the soul of business," he smiled.

Working for her boss, Frances had become a fellow creature of habit. Each morning, without fail, she arrived at the office at, if not before, 8:30 a.m.; she then checked with the agency for overnight messages and started her day by knocking out a new screen treatment from notes left by Roger. This first of the day's duties was finished by 9:00-9:15, at which time she walked down the street to The Copper Skillet, the coffee shop where she picked up Roger's breakfast—invariably, scrambled eggs on wheat toast. In the time they had worked together, she could not recall him ever failing to eat his breakfast while it was still warm. She glanced at her wristwatch as he stepped out of his convertible with the smile of a returning champion.

Some (Frances included) believed that Roger's smile was his secret weapon. Something about it was so cheering to others, so uplifting, not to mention so disarming, it was almost supernatural. However, the gift that sealed his deals—of both a professional and personal nature—was his voice. Roger's voice was deep in register, his enunciation crisp and perfect, and he always spoke in a low-key, measured and melodious cadence; it was a voice of reason, of guidance. He had the manner of a particularly gentle kindergarten teacher. This quality never left his voice, no matter what the circumstances.

"Scare-yyyy," Frances half-sang to herself as Roger walked past her into the office suite.

The walls inside agreed. To step inside the offices of The Corman Company was to be greeted by a gallery of framed posters for the most successful of Roger's brain children: *Not of This Earth, The Undead, A Bucket of Blood, The Little Shop of Horrors, War of the Satellites, The House of Usher, The Pit and the Pendulum, The Masque of the Red Death, The Tomb of Ligeia*—and a welcome gush of air conditioning.

It was a modest three-room suite: there was a private office for Roger, a smaller one that was sometimes made available to writers or other temporary associates, with Frances' reception area situated outside them. Roger strode purposefully through this space to his own office, his own desk, where he dropped into his patched leather chair and wolfed down his breakfast with juice. During his meal, Frances itemized what she had done since arriving and apprised him of whatever news was at hand—appointments, deadlines, even when he was due for a haircut.

"I'll look this over later," he said, draining his cup. "I'm due over in editing." The studio's editing department was a five-minute walk from the offices.

Frances was quietly astounded by the sheer industry of the man. Truth be told, she considered the education in film she had gained working by Roger's side the greater share of her salary. They were never not busy. One of the first things she had learned under his auspices was the magic formula necessary to keeping three pictures moving forward at once: Always have one in the editing room, one ready to shoot, and another in the typewriter. Past, present, and future—but, of course, it all had to be present tense for Roger.

She was prepared for this. On her desk waited three Anthora to-go cups filled with piping-hot coffee, huddled together with some apple and cinnamon Danish in a small cardboard box. She handed it to Roger, tapping each of the lids in turn: "Yours, black. These two are for Monte, cream and three sugars. He's been at it all night, poor dear. And," she added, tucking the morning *Times* under his arm, "your morning paper."

"Marry me, Frances," smiled Roger—an old routine.

"We're coming up on 9:40," she noted brightly, returning his serve. "Should you finish the edit before one, there just might be time for that—before your 2:00 interview."

Roger whistled a bar or two of "A Taste Of Honey" as he pushed his way through the front door.

CHAPTER 3

November 1966

IT WAS ON NOVEMBER 12, 1966 that fliers were stapled onto telephone poles around town and otherwise circulated, inviting people to head down to the Strip that night and join the protest outside Pandora's Box at the intersection of Sunset and Crescent Heights.

It's estimated that over a thousand heads accepted the invitation, while hundreds of additional curiosity-seekers clogged the Strip itself to rubberneck from their convertibles and motorcycles. Things pretty quickly got out of hand between law enforcement and the protesting element, some of whom were barely old enough to shave.

Among the protesters arrested on the evening of the first Sunset Strip riot was actor Peter Fonda. He hadn't really gone down to protest so much as to check out the scene. He took along his new Super 8 movie camera, just in case. Once he got there, he couldn't believe his eyes.

He found the Strip seething with squad cars. Stern warnings were being broadcast through bullhorns (*"The nightclub curfew is now in effect—anyone under the age of 18 years old remaining in the area will be arrested."*), cops in helmets and black leather gear marched shoulder-to-shoulder through masses of people—his own age or younger—carrying signs that pleaded "Give Us Our Freedom" and "Stop the Fascism." Staunch head that he was, he partook of some Michoacán before heading down and couldn't fucking believe he was in America, much less fucking California.

What caused all this tension? Some high-placed bankers on the prowl for martinis and pussy, getting bent all out of shape because their action was getting blocked by all the longhairs flocking to the Strip?

As he stood in the chaotic midst of it—business suits and Nehru jackets crossing like swords—Peter could sense the surreptitious shit in play, like the guilty resentment the Establishment felt in the presence of the generation their President was sending off to 'Nam by the thousand, indignant kids demanding their bite of life before they fell in line to die. Sometimes a familiar face—like Bobby Denver, or a face he knew from an old party or audition but couldn't quite place—would glance his way through the masses with an expression that was trying just as hard to place him. It was enough to ground Peter's mutual senses of belonging and outrage.

He filmed some young kids in their J.C. Penney clothes getting roughed up by the Man, for no worse transgression than being young and exercising their right to free speech. In a crush of humankind, he zoomed in on a cop being needlessly rough with a girl who had made the mistake of getting up in his face, and that's when Peter got himself slammed onto the hood of a parked car, cuffed, and shoved into a bus. His movie camera was confiscated. When the LAPD took his mug shot at the station, they had him hold a placard with his name and the designation "A1." He couldn't tell if he had been incarcerated or approved for the next chattel wagon to Saigon.

Long before it ever reached the youth culture, LSD had begun to influence the movies through early converts to its beneficial therapeutic effects, such as Cary Grant and Esther Williams.

In a September 1959 issue of *Look* magazine, Cary Grant spoke freely to its readership about his LSD experience:

"I've asked myself what do I want out of life? Beautiful women? Fantastic houses? No, I'm finding courage to live in the truth, as I want to live, not to impress other people. Possessions don't make you happy. I take my sunny and foggy days with me... All my life, I've been searching for peace of mind. I'd explored yoga and hypnotism and made attempts at mysticism. Nothing really seemed to give me what I wanted until this LSD treatment... [Now] I'm rid of guilt complexes and fears."

Esther Williams, America's favorite swimming star, was referred by Grant to his own therapist, Dr. Mortimer Hartman, and had a similar reaction. In the first chapter of her 1999 autobiography *Million Dollar Mermaid*, she would rhapsodize about her LSD experience—the first chapter of her life story, mind you. Under the influence of her first dose, Neptune's Daughter—seeking to unmask the cause of her own inescapable unhappiness—stripped naked before a full-length mirror and found the answer in her own reflection. There she beheld an image of herself, half-Esther and half-male; the latter portion of her reflection composed of her late brother Stanton, a radiant older sibling whose early death had denied him the stardom everyone had believed him born to, left his mourning sister to embody in his stead. For her whole life, for the sake of her grieving parents, Esther realized she had been living her life for two.

Needless to say, these early endorsements had everything to do with mental health and nothing to do with rock music, getting high, or the youth culture. Lysergic imagery began to surface in motion pictures with Federico Fellini's *La dolce vita* (1960) and John Huston's *Freud* (1962), both made by artists who had used the drug therapeutically and found themselves revolutionized by it artistically. Francis Crick would later confess that he first deduced the double helix formation of DNA—arguably the most important scientific discovery of the 20th century—under the influence of LSD. The drug was later popularized by Ken Kesey, who first took this and other hallucinogens as a test subject in a Top-Secret medical program conducted at the Menlo Park Veteran's Hospital—which happened to be covertly funded by the CIA. It was Kesey who, with a band of friends called The Merry Pranksters, had samples analyzed and reproduced to distribute freely among friends at a series of 1965-66 excursions and parties they dubbed "Acid Tests."

What was being tested at these impromptu gatherings was good old American conformity. The home base for the Pranksters' experimental happenings was moveable but primarily in the state of California, primarily Los Angeles and San Francisco. It was there that—in a desperate move to disadvantage his Republican opponent Ronald Reagan in the race for state governor—California governor Pat Brown would declare LSD illegal on 6 October 1966, a month or so before the riots. It was not to the advantage of a country that saw their young as military might in the war to safeguard capitalism to expose them to any agent that might reveal to them the universes awaiting detection in a drop of rain, in the breathing of trees, in the meaningless of materialism—in short, the sacred nature of life itself.

By taking LSD out of the hands of soul-seeking users and the medical professionals who also believed in it, California's self-interested politicians did indeed give rise to a more 'militant' youth, though not quite the kind they anticipated. The formula was out there, being duplicated and taken further by designer chemists like the legendary Owsley Stanley. The genie could not be put back into its bottle; its magic could only be turned into a crime.

And so came the outlaws.

While pausing at the prime real estate that was the red light at the intersection of Sunset and Miller Drive, Peter was taken aback by the presence of a new billboard overhanging the Tower Records building. It announced that now in production from American International was *Riot on Sunset Strip*, coming March 1967.

It was near midnight when he roared up to Harry Dean Stanton's modest, tree-shaded house, rounding the bend on his Harley. His engine metallically coughed to a state of silence—but the neighborhood itself was full of sounds. In one direction, he could hear a party going on, in another someone was playing a cut from the new Dylan album—the double one with the blurry cover photo. Mounting the steps, he looked in vain for any kind of doorbell and finally opted to jangle the wind chimes hung beside the mailbox.

No reply.

Tickling the stained glass triangles a second time, Peter was suddenly surprised by a generous sideways spritz of water from a garden hose. "Whoa!" he heard, as the flow was deflected.

On the other end of the blast, rapidly turning the hose off, was Jack

Nicholson, looking torn between great stoned embarrassment and even greater stoned amusement.

"Now here's a thing we got only in America," he explained, turning on the charm by affecting a redneck drawl. "You're out waterin' the petunias late at night and who should come a-callin' but Henry's boy!" He dropped the hose, ran up the steps to join him on the porch, extending a hand. As his handshake grew in vigor, so did an infectious smile.

There was something about him that was sort of irresistible; when the guy with the hose smiled, Peter's initial annoyance shifted gears to complete and utter forgiveness. It was like he already knew him, that they had met long ago somewhere—not at a Hollywood party, but in another time, another country, when they wore their hair and beards even longer than now, with sandals and flowing robes.

"I guess you're out lookin' for Harry?"

Peter cut to the chase. "No, man. You're Jack Nicholson."

"Yeah, so I've been told."

"I needed to see you. I couldn't wait. I just read your script."

"Wait a min—my script? Which one?"

"The one you wrote for Roger Corman's company. *The Trip*. When I finished reading it, I had to find you. I had to tell you."

"Uh . . . tell me what?"

"You've been hiding your most profound talent, man."

"Ain't been hidin' it," he admitted, "just nobody lookin' for it. Say, how'd you know I was here?"

"A mutual friend said you were crashing here."

"Crashing." Jack looked down at his shoes. "That's a good word for it."

"Where's Harry Dean?"

"Up in Lodi. Dennis Hopper got him a part in this Paul Newman picture he's makin'. Beg pardon, I'm a shitty host. C'mon in and check out the view. Just give me a sec to turn off the spigot over here."

After turning off the valve on the side of the house, Jack welcomed Peter inside with a tentative, mystified expression. They walked through a foyer and a kitchen to reach a back porch area that offered a surprisingly splendid and encompassing view of the lower neighborhood in the valley. Down there was the party he had overheard, new hippie royalty reveling around a bright blue swimming pool, and an uprising aroma that Peter—connoisseur that he was—judged to be Icebag. Jack gestured to a hanging wooden swing covered in slightly chipped white paint, but his guest was in a mood to pace. Jack took a seat himself and gave this certifiable movie star, the son of a movie legend, the space in which to talk.

"Seriously, man," Fonda paced while turning to him in earnest, "your script is the greatest thing I've ever read."

"Oh, yeah?"

"You found a way to express what's really going down today—who people really are, on both sides of the divide . . . how we're being controlled, and how it's really up to us as individuals and adventurers to liberate ourselves. You explain how acid is a way in—and why it's also a way out."

Jack gulped. "To tell you the truth, I wrote it so fast, I've been kinda scared to look at the pages again. You really liked it?"

"Look at it this way, dude," Peter smiled at him knowingly. "I read it in bed with my lady beside me. And I'm here."

"Right," Jack swallowed. "But you understood it? You didn't think it was a little—I dunno—*esoteric*?"

Peter stepped toward Jack and loomed over him dramatically.

"*It's easy now,*" he intoned, quoting the last line of the screenplay. "*Wait until tomorrow.*"

Then he broke character, as though the words had broken him. He blew air through his lips, his mind blown all over again. "Man, I understood every fuckin' word! You don't know what you've done! You've brought the French New Wave to the Pacific! You've put D.W. Griffith on mescalin!"

"I did?" he asked with an impish expression. "Well, won't the folks back home be proud!"

Jack sat there stunned . . . but was jolted from his daze by what sounded like a gunshot, followed by the equally unexpected sound of communal laughter. He sprang to his feet and crossed the back porch to its balustrade, and looked down into the party below. A tall, lanky longhair was firing a revolver into the empty pool, to the amusement of his friends, some of whom were naked.

Jack nodded down at the bacchanalia, as Peter solemnly joined him.

"My new neighbors, the Jefferson Airplane. They're in town makin' a record, rentin' John Phillip Law's pad while he's off in Rome makin' a movie."

"Oh, right," Peter noted. "With my sister."

"Yeah," muttered Jack, blue and wistful, "like I'm tellin' you." Sometimes it seemed like everybody in town was having a real career except him. He inhaled the sweet succor of the night air wafting up from further down the canyon. "I tell ya, they smoke a pretty good grade down there."

Fonda produced a fat joint from his jacket. "We have our own, man. Let's celebrate."

An hour or so later, the two of them were laughing, swaying on the porch swing, and cracking cans of Coors like a couple of long-lost brothers. By the time the neighborhood's soundtrack shifted from The Byrds' "Eight Miles High" to "(We Ain't Got) Nothing Yet" by The Blues Magoos, they reached the point of comparing notes on the one subject they had most crucially in common: Roger Corman.

It turned out that Jack had known Roger for close to 10 years. They first met in Jeff Corey's acting class, where the young producer-director enrolled to gain a better understanding of how actors worked. Notorious cheapskate that he was, it hadn't been lost on him that such experience would also allow him to step into scenes whenever someone was needed who didn't have to be paid. Corman had recognized Jack's talent and charisma and cast him in several pictures: *The Cry Baby Killer, The Little Shop of Horrors*, and *The Raven*; he was even the lead in a sorry-assed picture called *The Terror*. They all led nowhere. As Jack put it, "*The Terror* didn't even lead to the next Roger Corman picture."

Peter's relationship with Corman, on the other hand, was just the opposite. They had only recently met and made one picture together that, after years of white-bread roles in pictures he didn't like talking about, suddenly put him on the map as the most exciting American actor of his generation.

"I just did this biker thing with Roger," he mused. His words suddenly made Jack tighten up; he'd just been asked to play the lead in something called *Hell's Angels on Wheels*. But Jack was accustomed to keeping his feelings under wraps.

"And hit the jackpot, from what I heard," he grinned. "Congratulations. What was that like?"

"We had real Hell's Angels and Nancy Sinatra. No money, three weeks."

Jack, topping him: "Two days for *Little Shop of Horrors!*"

"Hey man, better that than *Tammy and the Schmuckface*."

They had a second joint going by now, and Peter took a deep toke. "So, who has Roger got to direct your script?" he asked, holding the smoke in. "You?"

"Oh, hell no," Jack answered. "He's gonna direct this one himself."

Peter coughed the smoke out. "Wait a minute. Roger's kind of a square dude, right? I mean, he knows his job . . . I actually learned a lot from him . . . but is he, like, the right guy to, you know, be making a movie about acid?"

Jack was way ahead of him: "Are you kidding? *The Wasp Woman . . . It Conquered the World . . . Not of This Earth . . . Teenage Caveman*?"

Peter began to grasp the enormity of what was going on here, or on the point of going on. "Oh, wow. Oh, WOW."

Jack took the joint. "It's not like, is he right for it?" He toked up. "It's more like, who better?"

Peter and Jack exchanged conspiratorial looks and giggled maniacally. After that, they fell quiet. Already, the two of them could be quiet with each other.

"Hey," Jack suddenly said, breaking the silence. "Did you see *The Times* today? They're reporting that film is a dying art form."

Peter cut short his stoned laughter.

"What's that?"

The relevant section of today's paper was folded right there on the swing between them. Jack handed it over, limply. "And with me just now poised for success. Read it and weep."

Peter unfolded the paper and saw, plain as day, a feature article in the Entertainment section with the portentous headline "*Film—A Dying Art Form.*"

He didn't read it, but he didn't have to. The advertisements framing the piece offered their own compelling evidence: *Doctor Doolittle*, *Namu the Killer Whale*, *Not with My Wife You Don't!*, *Lt. Robin Crusoe U.S.N.*, and *Thoroughly Modern Millie*—a musical set in the 1920s.

Peter cast the paper aside and returned to the porch rail, leaning on it with his back turned to Jack. Even so, Jack could see the tension in his shoulders. A moment later, Peter turned to face him with the conviction of a stone-cold revolutionary.

"I say we kill it or cure it."

CHAPTER 4

JUNE 1966

SCATTERED AT DIFFERENT POINTS in the darkened, clattering editing room were three stained to-go cups, one of them still holding enough Taster's Choice gone cold to float three cigarette butts. Roger was reading a handy *Time* magazine, glancing without particular interest at a story about Arnold Palmer's latest victory on the PGA Tour when his editor Monte Hellman spoke up.

"Hey, Roger. Check this out."

Roger rolled his chair into position to lean over the shoulder of his editor—blade-thin with a mop of dark, frizzy hair and long, jagged sideburns—and peered intently at the screen of a Steenbeck editing console.

"What are we looking at, Monte?"

The vigilant cutter lined up the precious moment he wanted to share: "Guest appearance by Peter Bogdanovich."

A foot pedal jerked the ribbon of dreams into action. On the Moviola screen, a baby-faced Bogdanovich—27 years old—was being assaulted by a Hell's Angels member at least twice his size. He landed heavily in the dirt, his round horn-rimmed eyeglasses flying from his face.

His bleary eyes gathering momentary glee, Monte wound the film back and forth, causing the celluloid image of Bogdanovich to flail and roll, roll and flail like a rag doll.

"Looks like he's really getting his ass kicked," Monte observed.

"In fact, he was," Roger informed him. "I found the Hell's Angels to be strongly in accord with approaches to performance favored by Method actors."

The light from the Steenbeck editing table played across Roger's intent gaze.

"Now, Monte," he continued, "about the funeral scene... There's a bit too much, I feel, of the widow getting raped in the church pew. AIP will never go for that, so I suggest cutting to something else. Maybe the priest getting beaten by chains... or perhaps that take of the two bikers emptying the bottles of whisky on Bruce's corpse."

"You got it," Monte grunted, firing up a Marlboro.

It was at this moment that the telephone rang. Roger grabbed it without taking his eyes away from the Steenbeck screen. It was Frances: "Roger? Your 2:00 interview from *Cahiers du Cinéma* is here..."

"Already? Where does the time go?"

"...and," she added, more portentously, "Gayle is on line three."

Roger's gaze remained glued to the Steenbeck. "Tell the magazine guy I'll be with him shortly. As for Gayle..."

His voice drifted off as he was drawn, mid-sentence, into a scene Monte had just finished cutting, a quiet dialogue between Peter Fonda and Nancy Sinatra, both dressed in biker garb.

NANCY: *Do you still love me?*
PETER: *I don't know.*

"Roger? What about Gayle?" Frances insisted. "Will you take the call or shall I give her a message?"

"Tell her... I can't now," he finally managed, hanging up. Then he patted Monte's shoulder and said, "Nice job."

The Wild Angels would continue to be fine-tuned in editing right up to the very last moment, but the film had been booked (in fact, well before shooting began) to open wide, in hundreds of theaters coast-to-coast, on August 10, with a World Premiere screening on July 20. A rough, temp-tracked cut had already been assembled as a courtesy to its executive producers, Samuel Z. Arkoff and James H. Nicholson of American International Pictures. However, that courtesy had yet to be conveyed.

Roger knew in his gut that the picture represented something boldly new, something considerably unlike the *Beach Party* films which, up till now, had embodied the company's idea of young people banding together for fun and adventure. He anticipated that Sam and Jim were going to have problems with this one. In fact, he wasn't quite sure of it himself, and he wasn't about to share it with them until he was.

In the meantime, he thought screening it for Etienne Lipschitz—a visiting critic from the French magazine *Cahiers du Cinéma*—might help to invest him with the certainty he usually felt by this point in a new picture's completion.

Frances had translated a few pieces of Etienne's work for him, which led Roger to anticipate the arrival of a rumple-suited, Gauloises-smoking acerbic in his early 50s with a fishy, Sartrean mien. But the guest who showed up at 2:00 couldn't have been more than 24 years old. He had dark, disarrayed hair, unevenly cut on the sides, dark glasses, an 8:00 shadow, and a smoke-fetid suit whose necktie was not only mismatched but somewhat bedraggled. When Frances introduced him to Roger, the young fan shook his hand reverently, as though one of Michelangelo's sculptures had stepped down off its marble platform to greet him. Roger apologized for speaking very little French—and offered Frances as an on-the-spot translator—but Etienne wouldn't hear of this; he insisted their encounter take place entirely in his *maître*'s language.

After a few minutes of preliminary conversation, Roger proposed to Etienne that they take a walk over to one of Columbia's screening rooms, where he could show him the rough cut of his new picture—a turn of events which the young critic had not expected nor dared hope for. They were now about 70 minutes into the feature and the Frenchman appeared to be completely under its admittedly brutal spell.

Frank Maxwell—a stocky, greying, buzz-cutted New York actor whom Roger had previously used in *The Intruder* and *The Haunted Palace*—was on the screen, standing at a church pulpit where a swastika flag had been draped behind him. He was playing the preacher at a small-town church that had been intimidated into hosting a funeral for "Loser," the character played by Bruce Dern.

"*Just what is it you want to do?*" he demanded of the mourning Angels.

Roger, his eyes fixed on Etienne from two rows distant, leaned forward to gauge his response to what was about to happen.

Peter Fonda was onscreen as the lead character, named Jack Black in Chuck Griffith's original screenplay, though this wasn't what he ended up being called in the film. In their first meeting, Fonda's only note was that he wanted his character to be renamed Heavenly Blues.

"Why Heavenly Blues?" Roger had inquired.

"A Heavenly Blue," Fonda explained, "is a morning glory that grows wild all around town, and if you take three or four hundred of their seeds, grind them up in a pepper mill and wash them down with a glass of water, you'll have one motherfucker hallucination."

It was at that moment that Roger first realized that theirs was destined to be an important collaboration. Now here he was, painted large on the screen—decked out in crypto-Nazi leather gear, acting not only as the spokesman for the Angels but for every teenager in the audience—neither old nor free enough to get his own kicks, but just the right age to be sent off by these buzz-cuts to die for their country.

Just what was it that they wanted to do?

"*We wanna be free!*" Fonda demanded, channeling Thomas Jefferson. "*We wanna be free to do what we want to do! We wanna be free to ride! We wanna be free to ride our machines without being hassled by The Man!*"

The Angels roared their approval as Father Maxwell grimaced, regarding these animals with the sour weariness of an ex-soldier who had fought the second World War for their kind.

"*And we wanna get loaded!*" Heavenly Blues shouted, adding a clause that was perhaps more to the point. "*And we want to have a good time! And that's what we are gonna do! We are gonna have a good time... We are gonna have a party!*"

As all hell broke loose onscreen, Etienne Lipschitz felt himself floating upward from his seat, ascending toward a whole new level of genre cinema Heaven. Roger could only see the back of his head, but he could tell from the feel of the room that the scene had played. He had a picture.

"And we wanna get loaded!" echoed Chuck Griffith, the screenwriter responsible for this masterpiece, before stuffing his mouth with a helping of moo goo from Mon Kee's Chinese Restaurant. Chuck was 35, going on 21, an unrepentant beatnik and beach bum who had written several of Roger's films, most notably *The Little Shop of Horrors*, but also this most recent one. His dishwater blond hair already showing its first traces of gray, amiably scruffy, and already at this point in time psychedelicized, Chuck was hanging out with his lunch in the projection booth. It had come to his attention that someone from *Cahiers* would be dropping by the office, so why not make himself available in case this person was open to quotes from the movie's author as well as the *auteur?*

"Where's Roger?" came a dry voice (or was it a wry voice?) behind him. Chuck turned to see Peter Bogdanovich—a fellow writer, hence the icing of his veins—stepping into the booth like he was stepping onto a yacht. His ascot was the color of the velvet curtains in a roadshow cinema.

"Showing a rough cut to *Cahiers du Cinéma*," Chuck answered.

"And we weren't invited? Say, is that Mon Kee's moo goo?"

Bogdanovich made a grab for a spare take-out carton sitting on a nearby table. Chuck thrust himself between it and the greedy outreach of his rival, willing to take a bullet for that moo goo, if necessary.

"First you rewrite my script, now you want to eat my moo goo?"

Bogdanovich folded his arms and keened an ear to the dialogue filtering through from the screening room. "I may have rewritten some pages," he said, "but I didn't touch your big speech."

Chuck, acknowledging the enormity of that favor, grudgingly conceded the leftovers and a set of snap-apart chop sticks. "Dig in . . . but *hands off the fortune cookies*!"

The lights came up in the screening room as the rough cut ended. There were no end titles on it yet, so its downbeat ending was more abrupt than it would be in theaters. Roger remained seated, once again taken aback by his own response to what he created. Granted, he was accustomed to watching it on the Steenbeck and every movie gained something when projected onto a huge screen; granted, it was a rough cut, close to 100 minutes as-is, and cutting it down could mean toning it down; and granted, he had been so focused on gauging Etienne's reaction that he had given no thought to what his own might be, but he found himself—as the film's creator—unaccountably squeamish.

Roger rose to his feet. Here's where those Jeff Corey acting classes really paid off.

"There you have it, Etienne," he smiled broadly at the critic. "Of course, the music was all temp track, and we're still tightening it up."

Etienne staggered up the aisle toward him.

"*Monsieur* Corman," he began, seizing him by the hand and the forearm, "this film is . . . *c'est absolutement . . . pardon* . . . it is absolutely remarkable."

"Oh?"

The critic looked incredulous. "But surely you must know this? What is most remarkable . . . is how much *reality*. Everything so real."

"Yes?"

"In your other films, *nothing* is real."

Roger thought he understood. "Well, yes. There was lots of outdoor shooting in this one, location shooting. One of the reasons I was drawn to this project is that I was beginning to find working indoors too confining. Let's take this back to my office, shall we?"

If the décor of Roger's reception area focused on his most commercial successes, his orderly (if not altogether clean) personal office was more specifically honoring of those films and achievements most important to him. Visible to Roger from his desk were the posters for "X"–*The Man with the X-Ray Eyes* (displayed near the Silver Spaceship Award it had won at the first International Festival of Science Fiction Film in Trieste, Italy) and *The Little Shop of Horrors*, a Chuck Griffith script he had somehow succeeded in filming in two-and-a-half days back in 1959. Hung behind his chair, thus visible from the seats used by visitors, was a framed poster for *The Intruder*. Not many people had seen it—not even Etienne, apparently—but it was the picture of which Roger was most proud. It was the film he wanted people to be thinking about when they looked at him across his desk.

The interview was now in progress. Roger was disappointed that his French visitor was only expressing interest in his horror and science fiction films, which he now felt were behind him, but with this new film as yet unreleased he could hardly expect otherwise. He wished he could wrap things up, but the best he could do under the circumstances was to offer up some of his stock prepared comments and answers. For example: "As an admirer of Poe and the writings of Sigmund Freud, I believe Poe's short stories anticipate Freud's own discovery of the subconscious." It wasn't a lie and the French gobbled up that sort of thing like *foie gras*.

"Let us then discuss these recurring motifs in your body of work," suggested Etienne. "The outsider. Sight. The fear of the Unknown. And the unseen. *Par example*, the alien vampire played by Paul Birch so brilliantly in *Not of This Earth*. He wear the dark glasses, like Ray Milland in the X. Or like Vincent Price in *Tomb of Ligeia*. They are allergic to light, punish by illumination."

"Exactly," Roger grinned, having no ready reply. He found himself fidgeting with an antique caliper kept on his desk as a paperweight.

"*Mon dieu!*" Etienne exclaimed. "Is that the actual claw of the Crab Monster?"

"Oh, no. He was much bigger. You've never seen a caliper? It's a device used by engineers. It measures the distance between the two sides of an object. A sentimental souvenir from my days at Stanford."

"Ah, *oui*! You know, I would like very much to know more about this side of you, to know and understand the real Roger Corman."

Gregarious just a moment before, Roger now felt a glimmer of discomfort.

"I want to know," Etienne continued, "where these marvelous ideas come from, what it is so deep inside you that is inspired by these ideas of mutation, of the apocalypse, about *love* on the threshold of apocalypse. I don't buy that you come back again to these themes, again and again, just for the *monnaie*."

The intercom buzzed, for which Roger was profoundly grateful. "Yes, Frances?"

"Sorry to interrupt, but we just had a call from Mr. Arkoff's office, inquiring as to when he and Jim might screen the picture."

Roger noted the shock on Etienne's face. "You see, Etienne? You really were the very first to see it."

"*The First Man on Earth*!" Etienne exclaimed, imagining how Roger Corman would entitle such an individual.

"How did he sound?"

"Impatient but flirty. In other matters, Gayle rang back. I told her you were in a meeting. Mr. Griffith asked me to relay that 'the author has gone back to Venice, if anyone cares.' Oh, and Peter Bogdanovich is out here, hovering."

Roger recognized a way out of the corner Etienne was fashioning. "Peter!" Roger exclaimed. "You should have told me, Frances. Please send him in!"

Wasting no time, Bogdanovich still managed to enter the room with an attitude of nonchalance.

Roger took this opportunity to rise from his chair and cross the room, meeting Bogdanovich halfway. "Etienne, meet Peter Bogdanovich. I'm sure you've heard of him. He writes about film for *Esquire*. He also assisted me on *The Wild Angels*. Peter, meet a fellow critic: Etienne Lipschitz of *Cahiers du Cinéma*."

Bogdanovich dropped his chin to his sternum, relaxed his facial features and slowly extended his hand. "How do you do?" he greeted, *à la* Hitchcock. Lipschitz, feeling his audience with the Master slipping away, forged ahead and moved the next chess piece of the interview.

"*Monsieur* Corman," he said, gesturing toward the poster on display, "I must know more about your masterpiece, "X"–*The Man with the X-Ray Eyes*! A man experiment on himself, yes?"

"Yes."

"This man, he take a drug and become heeper-sensitive. He see through all the layer. He see . . . a reality."

Roger was already halfway out the door.

"But *Monsieur*!" Etienne pleaded. "At least tell me this. What is reality . . . to Roger Corman?"

"Good question," Roger grinned. "Let me think about it. Have fun, you two!"

—.—

In an alcove of the reception area, Frances was loading a ream of paper into a Xerox machine. She saw Roger duck out of his office, looking darkly preoccupied. "Frances," he said, "walk with me."

They began walking down the inner corridor connecting to other offices. "Frances," he repeated, warming up to the subject at hand, "you're a woman..."

"Yes," she said, concealing her amusement.

"I mean, you're sensitive, right? You've got feelings."

"That's two for two, Roger. I'm a woman and I've got feelings. What are you trying to say?"

"To be perfectly candid, I'm a bit worried. Watching the film with this French fellow... I could tell he was quite taken with it, but I continue to feel somewhat unsure. Each time I see it, I get the feeling it's—well, kind of extreme. More so than I realized. More so than I really intended."

Frances called a stop to their forward movement and faced him. His expressions of crisis were rare in her experience and she wanted to give him her full attention and her response with both barrels.

"Roger, this movie should be rough. You saw how vicious those bikers were. You saw what they did to Peter. That was *real.* Toning it down, diluting the truth of what they were, what they are—it wouldn't be honest."

"Then you weren't upset by it?"

"Yes, but in a good way. If that makes sense."

Roger took her view into account and felt his internal scales shifting toward a more favorable balance. "We do see worse on the evening news, don't we?"

"Unfortunately, we do. And who brings us that news? Walter Cronkite, the most respected man in America."

Roger's mouth scrunched to one side. "True. But Walter Cronkite doesn't work for Sam Arkoff."

As the day wore on, it occurred to Roger that some of the insecurities he was feeling in regard to *The Wild Angels* might actually be some inverted form of the tremendous pride he felt in regard to what was taking shape, brought on by his malingering disappointment over his only box office disaster, *The Intruder.* The story of a rabble rouser sent to small towns to challenge and foment dissent regarding recently passed laws concerning racial integration in public schools, *The Intruder* had been an unusual picture for Roger in that it had been motivated by his own deeply held beliefs concerning the American Civil Rights movement. That night, he decided to run the picture for himself—just himself—in one of Columbia's screening rooms while taking intermittent chugs from a can of Metrecal, French Vanilla.

Onscreen was a promising young Canadian actor, William Shatner, soaking through a white linen suit in the sweltering summer heat of a place Roger's crew had dubbed "Arm Pit, Arkansas." Shatner was playing Adam Cramer, a rabble rouser sent by a John Birch-type society to a small Southern town obliged by newly passed integration laws to allow 10 black students to attend a none-too-welcoming, all-white high school. It was his mission to rile the whole town up to the point of reversing the law—but his efforts push them well beyond that into eruptions of violence.

"*Now you all know,*" Cramer was addressing a night rally of grumpy inbred faces, "*that there was peace and quiet in the South before the NAACP started stirrin' up trouble! But what you don't know... is that this so-called 'advancement of colored people'... is now—and has always been—nothing but a Communist front headed by a Jew... who hates America and doesn't make any bones about it either!*"

Roger leaned forward in his seat, still impressed by the force of Shatner's performance after four years.

"*Now let me ask you,*" the actor continued, somehow summoning the full authority of his voice though he'd come down with laryngitis the day before, "*do you people want niggers takin' over? And are you willing... to fight this down... into the last ditch... and keep fighting until it's over?*" His listeners—composed of the most sheepish and malevolent faces they had been able to find locally—cheered. "*Then I,*" Shatner railed to the heavens, "*am willing... to fight with ya!*"

Somewhere out there in the crowd, the liberal editor of the local paper challenged him by calling out: "*Why, Mr. Cramer?*"

I'll be damned, thought Roger. There was Frank Maxwell again—

playing the town's liberal newspaper editor! He'd forgotten he was in this picture. Same buzz-cut and everything!

But Shatner's character lived in the hope of having live bait step forward like that. He was prepared.

"*Why?*" Shatner yelled with incandescent bravado. "*Because I am an American, sir! And I love my country! And I am willin' to give my LIFE, if that be necessary, to see that my country stays FREE! WHITE! And AMERICAN!*"

The local yokels erupted into a frenzy of self-righteous bloodlust. The news editor scowled, disappointed in his town, in humankind. Roger leaned back in his seat as the film continued to unreel.

"It's such a powerful film," he heard Frances say from a couple of rows behind him. "You can't honestly think of it as a failure."

"I don't know. I was the hottest director in town and every studio in town was offering me *carte blanche* when I decided to make this picture. It was based on a book by Charlie Beaumont, so it wasn't like no one wanted to touch it—at least not in the book trade. But there wasn't a studio in town that was willing to work with me on this. I tried to appeal to them by trimming the budget to its barest minimum. I was only asking for $80,000 when my Poe pictures were costing me $250,000...Nobody wanted to make it."

"You wanted to show audiences something about themselves they didn't want to see. And as you know, 'If thine eye offend thee...'"

"That's right. They plucked me out."

"Yet you forged ahead. You took out a second mortgage on your house and made it anyway."

"I did."

"And now you have this picture, which you're proud of. What does this teach you?"

"That making movies is a business. It's best to keep your personal feelings out of it."

CHAPTER 5

JULY 1966 (I)

IT WAS THE FIRST FRIDAY after *The Wild Angels'* Wednesday opening. Roger Corman sat at his desk, gazing down at a small stack of current publications. More specifically, he was boring two angry holes in the one on top, a popular trade magazine for the motion picture industry. Pictured on its front cover were his associates Samuel Z. Arkoff and James H. Nicholson, the figureheads of AIP.

Sam, who had a background in entertainment law, was in his 40s, pumpkin-shaped, and almost never seen without a cigar; Jim, a former theater chain manager in his late 30s, was tall, pale, and wiry, with the formal, waxen demeanor of a mortician. They made a good team, Jim being the idea man and Sam having the huckster's mastery of bullshit to put them across. In this Associated Press photo, their jubilant expressions were in direct proportion to the headline, which boasted "'ANGELS' TOPS B.O. AIP'S BIGGEST EVER!"

Faced with this to-be-expected bit of self-promotion, Roger couldn't help remembering that neither of them had walked out of the film's initial rough-cut screening exactly beaming. Roger had felt some misgivings about the totality of the film's impact himself but hoped his partners might be encouraging, as Frances had been.

"What do you think of it, fellas?" he asked their unreadable faces.

"It's certainly an original picture, I'll give it that," ventured Jim, quickly turning to look out a window.

"Sam? I'm particularly interested in your response. It was you who suggested this subject matter."

Out came the cigar, a Partagas Robusto, followed by its aromatic effluvia.

"I'm glad you remember that, Roger, because I distinctly remember suggesting you make a motorcycle picture. I thought, perhaps naïvely, that you were on the right track when you said you had Nancy Sinatra and that she would be wearing boots for the first time in a picture."

"And?"

"You delivered that much, *mazel tov* on that. But what I was expecting was more along the lines of kids on summer vacation, having fun on their motorbikes, singing 12 new hit songs as they zoom along the highway. We need a movie for Fabian, but I never pressed him on you."

"Kind of a rough picture, Rog," Jim hedged.

"Rough is putting it mildly," Sam continued. "Let's see what we have here, besides Nancy Sinatra. We have our violence, we have our chaos, we have our swastikas . . . "

"Our" swastikas? Roger thought.

"You have them drinking beer after beer, sleeping out in the open, boy on girl, smoking that . . . loco weed, not to mention assorted defilements of churches, corpses, and graves. What, you don't consider this excessive for a picture?"

Roger took a moment. "I find the picture fully consistent with the reality that's out there."

"I think Sam was hoping for *The Mild Angels*," Jim said with a forced chuckle, hoping to relieve the atmosphere.

Sam fell silent, looking to the shapes sent out by his smoke for an answer. "Normally," he finally said, "I'd ask you to cut it but if we cut the fornicating thing, we'd have a two-minute picture. Roger, I would hope by now that you know AIP prides itself on being a *family-friendly* company—at least insomuch as some state censor boards still require this."

"Sam," Roger pointed out, "the kids who flocked to see *Pit and the Pendulum* when they were eight, nine, ten years old . . . they're teenagers now. Your audience is changing."

"Yes, but they still have parents, parents who want them to grow up right."

"This movie is going to upset some people, Rog," Jim piped in, straightening his striped tie.

Roger remained calm and rational. "Perhaps it should," he reasoned.

After they left, he could still hear Sam's hectoring voice outside the building, gradually diminishing as he crossed the parking lot to his waiting Oldsmobile Toronado.

Subsequently, they all learned an interesting lesson. One morning, Sam's office called to inform Roger that his picture was being released—absolutely uncut—under something new in AIP's history: a "Recommended for Adults" banner. It was something films like *Who's Afraid of Virginia Woolf?* and *The Pawnbroker* had brought into fashion.

The bottom of Roger's stomach dropped out when he first heard this, because the last thing he had intended to do was to turn his back on his established audience. However, it turned out to be exactly what was called-for, because the film not only became the stuff of big box office but the stuff of newspaper editorials, conservative *and* liberal, and led to heated discussions within the home between parents and teens.

In its first two days of release, *The Wild Angels* more than tripled its original $360,000 investment and, according to Roger's canny calculations, was on track to accrue as much as $5-6,000,000 in box office receipts.

He should have been overjoyed, festive, gleeful as his movie topped *Variety*'s list of the Week's Top Grossing Films week after week—but instead, he felt annoyed. Annoyed that Columbia, who had provided him with this office on their lot and all the perks of being one of their directors under contract, had shown no interest in releasing it. And what did they release instead? *The Silencers* with Dean Martin, *The Trouble with Angels*, *The Man Called Flintstone*. If this was the baseline for motion pictures, where could he go from here?

"Roger, what am I going to do with you?"

He looked up and saw Frances framed in the office doorway, looking very chic. She had evidently changed into something showier, wowier, after putting in a day's work in less distracting office apparel.

"I can't wait to find out," he responded, playing their little office game.

"You know what I mean," she chided. "You have the Number One film in the country—in relation to cost, probably the biggest film success of the year. Shouldn't you be out celebrating?"

He took a slug of Metrecal and held up the can. "Strawberry. I *am* celebrating."

"I do wish you could learn to enjoy yourself."

"Figuring out my next move *is* enjoying myself," he said, gesturing to the stack of magazines. "What do you have planned for this evening?"

"It's Movie Night. The new Hitchcock, *Torn Curtain*—or *Paradise, Hawaiian Style*, the latest Elvis. We haven't decided yet."

"'We'? How intriguing."

Frances rolled her eyes. "Agnes and Emily from the next office over. Girls' Night Out."

Roger took a pencil and made a note. "*Girls' Night Out—may* have title potential." He looked up from his scribbling. "My advice is, Go with the Hitchcock."

Frances sighed. "I'll make the case, but Agnes loves Elvis. Ta!"

Time passed, objects in the heavens moved, earthly shadows lengthened, and the sky began to darken, yet Roger Corman continued to occupy the same space at his desk—not unlike the gnomon of a sundial. He had moved past the industry journal and was now turning his attention to the other current periodicals in his stack. Each magazine cover seemed to portend immense cultural change, whether it was politics, teenagers, or the race to the moon.

The cover of *Time* asked the provocative question, "Is God Dead?"

Newsweek's cover concerned itself with the subject of "LSD and the Mind Drugs."

However, at the moment, Roger found himself drawn to the magazine at the bottom of the stack, which happened to be *Playboy*. He leaned back in his chair, put his feet on his desk and let the centerfold tumble open. A doe-eyed brunette was raising an angora sweater above her breasts, her maroon slacks teasingly unzipped.

"I told you he'd be hard at work," came a voice from the doorway.

Standing there were Peter Bogdanovich and Chuck Griffith—an unlikely duo, but not without prospects. Roger laughed, refolded the magazine and sat up straight.

"Have you guys seen this?" he asked, holding up the industry journal. "How does it feel to have written the Number One film in the country?"

The two scribes exchanged looks and knew they finally had something they could agree about.

"We wanna have a good time!" they chanted in unison. "And we wanna get loaded!"

Peter's car was in the shop, Chuck had found his way over to Gower using his thumb. Roger, having more to celebrate than either of them, left his car at the office and the three of them headed off by taxi to the phantasmagorical bazaar that was the Sunset Strip on a Friday night in the summer of 1966—the Summer of Foreplay before the Summer of Love.

En route to the first place that looked promising, they saw an enormous billboard for *The Wild Angels* and decided to stop right there, just a few steps away from a trendy new nightspot called The Bead Game. Roger got out first, leaving it to Chuck and Bogdanovich to settle the $1.75 fare between them. He busied himself studying the Op-art posters arrayed either side of the entrance, the colors so intense they looked wet to the touch.

"Fellas," Roger said, while examining the posters, "I think this is a vegetarian restaurant."

"That's not a menu," Chuck explained. "Electric Prunes and Ultimate Spinach are the bands playing here tonight."

The interior of the club was piquantly disorienting. Once inside the funhouse door, patrons were met by walls painted with whorling patterns like enormous fingerprints. The lines and the backgrounds were conflicting colors that collided in a vibrating effect. The walls bordering the zig-zag corridor, leading deeper inside, were bombarded with black light and made one feel they were inside a large pulsating heart whose pulsations emanated from the band onstage.

All this was very new to Roger, who had always been a steak and martini kind of guy. At the same time, he had always identified with the Outsider in his art, and Chuck was leading the way like he'd been here many times before, so he figured, *What the hell, bring it on.*

As they turned the final corner of the point of entry, the enclosed space seemed to explode outward into a space-age version of what Roger would have called a nightclub. They were greeted by pretty hostesses fragrant with jasmine and patchouli and guided past a dance floor and dining area to the best booth in the place. Normally, this would require at least a $50 bribe—beyond the means of both Chuck and Bogdanovich, but the latter happened to mention that the gentleman in the cardigan was the director of *The Wild Angels* and, tonight, that did the trick.

Ultimate Spinach—a band from Boston, though you could never tell it from their strangely gothic ethereal sound—was onstage performing "Ballad of the Hip Death Goddess." Blobs of colored oil-and-water wobbled and throbbed on light-show screens arranged around the sensorium. The three men were guided to a VIP booth, where they sat like birthday boys, dazzled by everything, Roger looking particularly stimulated.

He tapped Bogdanovich's shoulder and shouted in his ear to be heard. "Nice Escher painting over there!"

"That's not an Escher, Roger," Bogdanovich deadpanned. "That's the way to the john."

As if summoned up from the loping depths of the song's bass line, an attractive girl with shoulder-length dark hair emerged from the throbbing darkness to take their drink orders. "I'm Robin," she said. "I'll be your server this evening. What'll you gentlemen have?"

First, all three of the men felt like having a good look at the fantasy vision before them. Robin was wearing a white linen blouse with puffy shoulders under a blue gingham apron dress, like the one famously worn by Dorothy Gale of Kansas, only much shorter. This misleadingly wholesome ensemble invited everyone's eyes to slide down her black cross-hatched nylons past her knees to a pair of ruby metal-flake go-go boots.

"Tequila Sunrise," said Chuck, holding up his hand like a boy in class.

"Dry Manhattan for me," voted Bogdanovich, arching his index finger. "And this"—he added, patting the central member of their gathering on his shoulder—"is our Guest of Honor this evening, so give him whatever he wants. Chuck and I will haggle over the check later."

Chuck rolled his eyes and made plans to duck out early.

Robin turned her best guest-of-honor smile toward Roger. "What's the occasion?"

"We're the Wild Angels!" sang out the two on Roger's either side.

"And who's your Guest of Honor?" she asked, openly flirting with him.

"I guess I'm the *Mild* Angel," Roger grinned. "I'll have a dry gin martini—olives, straight up. And since this is a special occasion, make it Bombay Sapphire."

Robin's eyebrow arched approvingly.

Ten minutes later, she returned with the drinks and placed them on the table with a flourish of ceremony. "Tequila Sunrise... Dry Manhattan... and, for the Man of the Moment, our best dry gin martini—olives, straight up. I'll be keeping my eyes on you boys, but if you don't see me when you're ready for the next round, just send up a flare."

She then curtsied and danced away, leaving Chuck and Bogdanovich to toast Roger and *The Wild Angels* and their shared moment of great success. "And here's to my wild colleagues," he added, "without whom I couldn't have done it!"

Bogdanovich rubbed his shoulder with pained nostalgia: "You can manage some incredible things when your writer doubles as a stuntman."

"*Re*-writer," Chuck insisted. He cast a tequila-infused eye around the club. "Well, Mr. Stuntman... see anyone here you might take a fall for?"

"Possibly," Bogdanovich allowed, "but it would have a somewhat deleterious effect on my marriage."

"Oh, bosh," Chuck declared. "Marriage is just a state of mind." He looked at Roger and saw that he was completely astounded by the sights and sounds abounding. "Not like the Smoke House, is it, Rog?"

"I should say not!" He didn't elaborate.

"Come on, open up, be gregarious in your moment of triumph! What's on your mind?"

"My mind?" Roger asked brightly, snapping back into place.

"Yeah, you know, that thing you use to make all those shrewd business deals you're known for."

"Oh, I don't know. I don't have an idea for the next picture yet."

"Screw the next picture," Chuck suggested suggestively. "Sitting there, right now. 'Top o' the world, Ma!' What would you like to do?"

Roger looked across the room at the girl named Robin, wending her way with drinks through the midway, delivering them and taking new orders and looking altogether enchanting. Roger wondered, could he make her look in his direction simply through his powers of concentration?

"Chuck," he said, "that's an entirely different kind of decision—and I'm not sure if it's mine to make."

Chuck followed Roger's line of vision and raised a hand, signaling to Robin for another round.

Bogdanovich was now one Dry Manhattan down. "Roger, don't give us that humble crap. You've got this town by the shorthairs. Just decide what you really want and you can have it."

"Okay," he decided, as Robin returned, pen and pad in hand. "I'll have another gin martini. But this time," he added, using his voice to its full effect, "just have them *whisper* the word 'vermouth' over the gin."

Robin smiled back: "You got it."

And so, time passed into the wee hours on rafts of drinkipoos, Roger sitting in the middle of the booth with a nice buzz while Chuck and Bogdanovich—bookending him like the miscast Angel and Devil of his conscience—were besottedly committing the sin of openly discussing his Art in his presence. Somewhere, somehow, this discussion metamorfizzled into an equally open discussion of his dating habits. They were on Clouds Nine and Eight, and in his chummy good company, so it seemed like fair game to talk about him, around him, forgetting that he was their primary (maybe only) means of keeping a foot in the film business. Fortunately, Roger—who enjoyed being assessed—didn't mind that these two were mining territory his shrink had yet to pick at.

Here was Bogdanovich: "Have you ever noticed his tendency in casting to go from blonde to brunette and back again? It's like the hair is more important to him than who it's—you know—growing on."

"Did you notice that scene in *Tomb of Ligeia* where the fair-haired heroine finds the dark hair in her hairbrush?" countered Chuck. "Brrrrr!"

"Yeah, Roger," Bogdanovich slurred, "what's all that about? Is there some kind of struggle going on inside you, between all these blondes and brunettes?"

So, they were finally involving him in the conversation.

"I wouldn't exactly call it a struggle," he smiled gamely.

"It's that or they're either too tall or too short, too brainy or too dumb," Chuck argued. "He's picky!"

"The word is 'selective,'" Roger corrected him.

Bogdanovich pled his case: "Last month, Chuck... Get a load of this. I fixed him up with this beautiful brunette. She had a body that wouldn't quit. A *summa cum laude*—from Yale, no less. On top of that, she just sold her first book of short stories to City Lights! A goddess! And he dropped her like a hot potato."

Chuck's brow furrowed. "Because?"

"She was a Republican," explained Bogdanovich.

Roger perked up. "Have you guys seen what's going on in Vietnam?"

"That ain't just Republicans, Rog," said Chuck.

"Point taken," Roger allowed. "Anyway, that is not the reason I stopped seeing her."

"Then WHY?" Bogdanovich demanded to know.

"That's easy chum," Chuck offered. He started rattling off movie titles. "*Pit and the Pendulum... The Wasp Woman... Swamp Women... Rock All Night*... You might as well say 'Freud's Greatest Hits.'"

Even Roger laughed.

Bogdanovich mused. "Better not bring up *Attack of the Crab Monsters*."

Chuck spat up his drink and slapped the table.

"There is a perfectly valid..." Roger began to say, halted in mid-sentence as a hornet-like electric guitar shimmer pierced the play of colored lights. The Electric Prunes had taken the stage with their hit song "I Had Too Much To Dream (Last Night)."

Last night your shadow fell upon my lonely room
I touched your golden hair and tasted your perfume
Your eyes were filled with love the way they used to be
Your gentle hand reached out to comfort me

Robin reappeared from the shadows as thunderous drums rocked out—*"Then came the dawn!"*—unabashedly locking her eyes with his. Without ever looking away, she crossed the full length of the room back to their VIP booth, every scissoring step conveying the weight of rock 'n' roll.

"Last call," she said. "Is there anything else I can provide for you gentlemen?"

Roger smiled.

After Chuck and Bogdanovich bade him a fuzzy farewell and retreated back into their private lives, Roger remained behind, wanting to savor another martini—this time with a twist... named Robin. In her Oz outfit, she had led him away from the very public booth he occupied to a more intimate, privately situated VIP booth. Roger watched the roadies dismantle the Electric Prunes' equipment until Robin returned, now out of uniform and dressed in her own very appealing street clothes. Her return pleasantly coincided with pre-recorded music of a gentler yet spicier lilt—Sergio Mendes and Brasil '66. The volume was just right to encourage conversation.

"You really work in the movies?" she asked. "I would never have figured you for the type."

"Why not?"

"You're way too—I don't know—shy or something. I had you pegged as an accountant."

"I studied to be an engineer, actually." He glanced at his wristwatch. "Look, I was wondering..."

"I'm wondering too," she interrupted. "How many times do you check your watch in an evening?"

"I didn't mean to offend you. I just..."

Robin leaned in for a sip of his martini. "I'm not offended."

She held his gaze as she stole the sip. At that moment, her frankness was complemented by a passing overhead light which combed the length of her hair in an iridescent trail of swimming paisleys.

"When do you get off work?"

She bit her lower lip. "Two hours ago."

Another album in the stack dropped onto the turntable and another serving of bachelor pad Easy Listening wafted from the stereo. Scattered near the turntable were various album covers: Mr. Acker Bilk's *Stranger On the Shore*, Herb Alpert's *Whipped Cream and Other Delights*, The Dave Brubeck Trio's *Time Out* featuring "Take Five"—all instrumentals.

On the other side of the room, Roger lay stretched out on the living room sofa as Robin straddled him. She was now in her street clothes (or most of them), her back unzipped, her skirt hiked up over her thighs. Go-go boots lay crumpled on the floor.

"Wait a sec," she said, interrupting a deep kiss. She reached for her purse on the floor and couldn't quite reach it. She then wriggled off Roger's lap, which caused him to yelp.

"You okay?"

"Old tennis injury," he explained.

He watched her rifle through her bag till she secured a small tinted container of pills.

"What are those?"

"An ingenious invention of Drs. Pincus and Djerassi. One a day keeps the babies away."

"That's very thoughtful of you."

"I'm no Girl Scout but I believe in being prepared. Where can I get some water?"

Roger indicated the kitchen. "There's some clean glasses in the dishwasher."

As she stepped out of the room, he readjusted his aching back and reflected briefly on the responsibilities of dating. He heard her rummaging through the dishwasher and closing it. A moment or two later, Robin sauntered back, sipping a glass of water while casually inspecting the adornments of Roger's living room.

Still not fully aware of who Roger was, had she known better, she might have found his pad rather Spartan for a man of his accomplishments. It was almost too small to be called a house; spending so little time at home, he considered spatial extravagance wasteful. He also didn't own a lot of "stuff"; he wasn't yet ready to feel comfortable; all he really needed was a place to hang that bucket hat of his, where he could also grab it fast and head back out the door whenever the opportunity arose to be productive.

He had lived in this house for several years, but its predominantly white décor could still be termed "unlived-in," apart from its bookshelves. There an impressive number of hardcover and paperback volumes were meticulously arranged according to subject and genre, size and chronology. Here and there you might also see the occasional memento or geegaw—like the old-school painting of an elegant clipper ship displayed near the kitchen entrance—but nothing that would reveal much about him to chance visitors. This was fitting, as there were people who had known Roger since his first years in Hollywood who would tell you they still didn't really know him; the more discerning ones would add that they were also unsure how well he really knew himself. "But who does, Dad?" they might append, "I mean, really?"

Roger's sole domestic concession to his public self was a framed poster for *The Day the World Ended*—not his first film as a director, but the one generally regarded as the first real Roger Corman film. It was the first film he made that was meaningful to him, his first personal statement that made some seriously impersonal money. With that film, a humble little company known as American Releasing Corporation became American International Pictures.

"You've got a real interesting hideout here," Robin apprised. "Kinda square, but... kinda cool too."

She walked back toward the sofa and looked for more clues to this kinda square, kinda cool guy in the items laid out across the top of a vaguely futuristic, glass-topped coffee table. There was a short, neat stack of film scripts, a copy of *Playboy Party Jokes*, a somewhat rumpled months-old issue of *American Cinematographer*, and a "Pat Brown for Governor" bumper sticker.

"So," she probed, picking up the bumper sticker and flashing it back at him, "is this your guy?"

Roger had turned onto his side, resting his head on his hand. "Hard to say," he answered. "I'm feeling a little uncommitted about things right now."

"Hard to say, or you know better to talk politics on dates till . . . you get to know each other . . . a little better?" Robin asked provocatively.

Roger laughed without making a sound, and his date seated herself on the floor, quite close to him.

"Everybody I know at school is deeply committed—one way or another," she said, picking up and flipping through Roger's copy of *Playboy Party Jokes*. It was full of cartoons of a tiny brunette clad only in black stockings, known to the magazine's readers as Femlin.

"School?"

"Yeah, I've been auditing classes at UCLA," Robin explained. "You know. Improving my mind."

"A worthy cause," Roger smiled. "What classes?"

"Oh, 'Narrative Consciousness in Fiction and Film.' We read books, watch movies. We did Kafka last week. *The Trial*. Orson Welles." Her eyes widened as she added: "Pretty mind-blowing."

Roger raised his eyebrows, impressed.

"The gentleman looks surprised," Robin teased, closing the *Playboy* book and tapping it indicatively. "Thought I was just another dumb bunny, huh?"

"Not at all. I hope they're teaching you some Bergman, as well."

"They are," she answered. She put her glass down and slowly began to climb on top of him. "*Smiles of a Summer Night*," she said—and smiled. "*Sawdust and Tinsel*," she said, letting her dark hair tickle and buffet his face. She lightly kissed his chest, then his chin, and then she looked up with a piquant expression of surprise. "*Summer with Monika*." She pressed her lips to his cheek six quick times, and then, after saying "*The Seventh Seal*," lowered her lips softly and warmly onto his.

CHAPTER 6

July 1966 (2)

PEOPLE CAN BE REDUCED TO simple generalities of all sorts, but one of the most significant dichotomies in the human animal is the favoring of logic over emotion, and vice versa. In Italy, people regard this as a regional phenomenon; they will tell you that the more reasonable, academic and systematic Italians are native to the northern regions, while the more emotional people of their country, the ones who scream and gesticulate and throw bread rolls, hail from the south.

For as long as he could remember, Roger's mind had strongly favored the logical model, being keenly attuned to the solving of problems. One of the things he loved most about the film business—second, in fact, only to the vast amounts of cash that could be generated from a little money and a lot of initiative—was that it offered him an almost endless number of problems to solve.

Therefore, when he made his first appointment with a psychiatrist—in 1960, around the time of his first Poe picture's immense commercial success—he was not looking for help so much as understanding, illumination. He didn't consider himself broken, but there were things about his own behavior, about his methodology, he didn't fully understand, and he was curious to know himself better.

Dr. Roberta Xavier MD, his psychiatrist, had come to the conclusion quite early on in their therapy that Roger was neither mentally ill nor socially maladjusted, but was probably guilty to an extent of taking narcissistic interest in his own interior processes—but Dr. Xavier was, in all fairness to both parties, a Hollywood psychiatrist and saw a lot of this among her well-salaried patients. Roger, like her less serious cases, met with her only once a week: Tuesday afternoons at 2:30.

The room was dusky in the mid-day light, which Dr. Xavier liked (the better to encourage introspection), and adorned with small abstract paintings and knick-knacks she had collected in her travels, no two things alike, the better to spark associations of thought in her patients. Roger was always offered the choice of a comfortable chair or a full-length sofa. Today he had chosen the sofa but sat upright on it, tapping his foot in a way that was obviously not to music.

"I've heard you have a new movie coming out."

"I always have a new movie coming out. One in theaters, one in the editing room, one in the typewriter. At least that's my goal."

"There was an interview in the paper with your boss."

"Boss?" Roger asked. "I don't have a boss."

"A Mr. Arkoff?"

"That's Sam. He's not my boss."

"Sorry. I admit, there's a lot I don't know about the film business."

"Sam's a distributor. I made the picture. He bought it from me, the right to package and resell it. He buys pictures, he doesn't make them. He feels they're his. He loves attention, blowing smoke with that cigar of his. I think he's only in the picture business to put his name on as many things as possible."

"And you're not?"

"I love signing a picture, actually," Roger said, adjusting the lens trained on him. "But even more than signing it with my name, I like signing it 'Problem Solved.'"

"Does it always work out that way?"

"Not always. A few years ago, I made a picture in Ireland called *The Young Racers*. It was about the Grand Prix."

"The one that's in theaters now, with that guy from *Maverick*?"

"No," Roger said flatly, throwing a quick look over his shoulder. "Mine came out in 1963."

"Ahead of the curve. Go on, I'm sorry."

Roger continued: "The storyline was the usual soap opera involving the drivers and their girlfriends, building up to a big climactic race. On the day we were going to shoot this big race, one of the stunt drivers failed to show up. So, I ended up driving in his place. The thing is, I was supposed to lose. But once I got out there and drove a few circuits, I found myself in the lead. I started winning. And suddenly, winning became more important to me than getting the scene."

"Did you win?"

"I did. I won the race. But I lost the day. I had to restage and reshoot the whole thing. My producer was furious."

"Mr. Arkoff?"

"Me. I produced it. Sam was just the distributor."

"So, you were working against yourself!" Xavier savored. "That's an odd kind of competition, don't you think?"

"You tell me."

"Ah, but my job is to get *you* to tell *me*! Is there anyone with whom you feel competitive in your day-to-day life?"

"Yes, if keeping an eye on other people's box office returns counts. But that is as it should be, given they are 'the competition.'"

"Who do you see as 'the competition'?"

"I don't know... Bert Gordon, William Castle, Mario Bava—people who do more or less what I do."

"Which is?" the doctor asked.

"Making actors rise out of coffins."

"Is that how you see your job description? Making actors rise out of coffins?"

"Not anymore. I believe I'm moving past that now."

"Are you aware of anyone else in your business who is doing what you're doing right now?"

"You mean, talking to a psychiatrist? Probably each and every one of them."

"You know what I mean."

"Not at the moment. But, in my business, it's inevitable. There is always somebody right behind you, waiting to see what you're going to do next, so they can do it with far less money—or in the case of *Grand Prix*, far more money."

"So, you work faster, staying ahead of the pack. Do you feel competitive toward Mr. Karloff?"

"Karloff? I think you mean Arkoff."

Dr. Xavier smiled apologetically.

"Either way," Roger summarized, "no."

"Siblings? You have a brother, don't you?"

"Yes, but . . . "

"What does he do?"

"He's a film producer."

"Don't you find that *interesting?*" Dr. Xavier asked brightly.

"I find that obvious. I'm not here to explore the obvious."

"You and I seem to continually come up against these walls of resistance. They're there when we discuss your family members. When we discuss your relationships with women, or your resentment of Mr. Karloff."

"Arkoff."

She apologized this time with a dismissive gesture. "Your fundamental problem, as I see it—is that you have no real interest in changing."

"But I embrace change!" Roger objected. He started counting examples on his fingers. "I'm always meeting and dating new women. I buy a new sports car almost every year. I haven't even worked with Vincent Price in over a year!"

Xavier could no longer conceal her exasperation. "Mr. Corman, have you learned anything at all from the time you've spent in analysis?"

Roger checked his wristwatch—*did he have time to answer?* He didn't want to start and get cut off.

"I've learned that B-movies and psychiatry have something very much in common."

"Oh?"

"They both give you about 60 minutes to tell your story."

"Are we ever going to get any closer to *your* story?"

Roger checked his watch once more. Ten seconds to go. He promptly rose from the couch, pinched the collar of his sport coat, lifting it from the coat rack, and opened the door.

"It might help if you served popcorn."

With that and a smile, Roger was gone—slightly ahead of schedule.

Since his date with Robin, Roger had gone out (and stayed in) with a variety of women, alternating between blondes and brunettes as was his tendency.

On this particular morning, his companion was Iris, an actress he'd met on the Columbia lot. She was hoping to make it in pictures but, for the moment, was stuck in one-shot series appearances and pilots for Screen Gems. She had just auditioned for, and failed to get, a role in an episode of *The Monkees* that went to Katherine Walsh. She was a comely, flax-haired woman; though only 10 or so years Roger's junior, she comported herself in ways one might associate with girls of somewhat greater distance. They quickly discovered they were nothing like one another, but opposites sometimes attract. She was as mystified by the clothes in Roger's closet as he was intrigued by her array of tie-dyed halter tops and appliquéd bell bottom jeans. Moreover, accustomed as Roger was to working, Iris had an unrepentant allergy to Monday mornings.

It was now such a Monday morning, a persecuting postscript to a long and luxuriant weekend spent behind drawn shades and closed curtains. Iris was not feeling her best as she rode shotgun in his Mercedes convertible along Santa Monica Boulevard with Herb Alpert's peppy "Spanish Flea" tooting from the 8-track deck.

"Roger," she whined. "Don't you have any rock and roll?"

"What's the matter, honey? Don't you like Herb?"

"I could use a little herb," Iris groaned. Then she remembered what she was carrying and started rummaging around inside her handbag.

In a matter of moments, she had located her quarry: a strip of blotter paper. Mistakable at a glance for a length of S&H Green Stamps, it was broken up into a sequence of squares adorned with the image of Mr. Horsepower—a feisty, squinting woodpecker clenching a pair of stogies between its teeth. Iris tore one off, touched it to her tongue for a few seconds, then flicked the paper away to be carried off on the California breeze.

At exactly 9:30, Roger glided once again into his parking spot at the studio, where Frances stood as usual waiting to greet him. She hadn't been expecting the young woman whose clothes reminded her of a toucan, but she had seen enough in the few years she had worked with Roger to not be surprised. Besides, the morning's mood was too glorious to be denied.

"Good morning, Frances!"

"We couldn't ask for a better one," she beamed.

"Really? Why is that?"

"Roger, *please*. *The Wild Angels?* Have you not seen the weekend box office figures?"

"We've been, uh, busy."

"Biggest weekend box office yet. People are not just talking—they're *still* talking."

Roger was pleased, but his pleasure was tempered by the knowledge that Sam and Jim would be getting restless. If he didn't come to them with something soon, they would come to him with something else—something he wouldn't want to do.

Frances was looking at him with a strange expression, one he'd never seen on her face. A gentle wind was stirring her hair.

"What is it, Frances?"

"Can't you *feel* it?"

"Feel what?"

"I don't know what it is, but there's definitely something... *bewildering* in the air!"

Iris spun around in response and looked warily at the sky. "I just have a feeling," Frances continued, "—call it intuition—that something very special is coming into being, and your film is part of that." She warily extended her hand to Roger's new friend. "Frances Doel."

Roger piped up. "That's right, you two haven't met! Frances, this is Iris." Iris momentarily beamed back to Earth and shook the waiting hand.

"How do you do?" Frances greeted her, to which the wandering waif answered either "Hi" or "High." As the three of them entered the Corman Company offices, Frances turned to other current events:

"Did you read the latest about Peter Fonda's marijuana arrest?"

"I did. I think he's getting a raw deal."

"Meanwhile, *The Wild Angels* is getting a massive windfall of free publicity. Oh," Frances added apologetically, "you didn't mention bringing a guest, so I'm afraid there's just one Copper Kettle breakfast on your desk. Shall I go for another?"

Roger turned cheerfully to Iris: "We'll split mine!" But he didn't find her standing nearby, where he expected her to be; she had lagged behind and was caught up in the strange imagery arrayed to greet visitors from the framed posters on the walls.

The Young Racers—two half-naked lovers lay entwined on a race track as a speeding Lotus comes rocketing toward them. "A Little Death Each Day... A Lot of Love Every Night!"

A Bucket of Blood—"He Lived For His Art... And His Art Was Murder!"

Not of This Earth—a likeness of Beverly Garland clawing her face in horror.

Iris turned to Roger and Frances. "Oh... my... God," she announced. "You won't believe what I just did."

Please don't say you wee'd yourself, Frances silently prayed.

"I left my purse in your car. And I left my glasses in my purse. Can I have your keys? To put inside your lock to get inside your car? To get my purse and get inside my purse and find where I left my glasses?"

"It's a convertible."

Iris continued looking at him expectantly, so Roger reached into his chinos and tossed her the keys, which she caught with what might be described as cosmic precision.

"Be right back," Iris promised. With each step toward the door, she got lost all over again in a different poster. Halfway to the door, she abruptly stopped, looked down and exclaimed "I'm not barefoot! Good!"

Once she was out the door, Roger and Frances exchanged looks. "Do you think she'll find her way back?" Frances asked.

"I don't know what's got into her," Roger mentioned, semi-worried. "I think you must intimidate her. It's that Oxford accent of yours."

"Can't be helped. Actually, Roger, I'm fairly certain she's on something."

"'On' something?"

"Something chemical? Of the psychedelic variety? A mushroom from the *psilocybe* family perhaps, or a spot of lysergic acid diethylamide? You know. LSD."

Inquisitively, Roger inched toward the exit and cast his gaze into the parking lot, where he saw Iris digging around in his back seat, her delectably mini-dressed rump, long tanned legs and sandaled feet all hanging clownishly out the door.

Frances broke the silence, standing directly behind him: "It's very popular right now. They say it transforms the way you see and feel."

The office telephone began to ring.

"Corman Company," Frances answered.

"How ya doing, Franny?" came the unmistakable voice of Sam Arkoff—the voice of a seasoned carnival barker.

"Quite well, Sam," she said, tolerating the nickname. "I know how *you* must be doing today."

"Hello, hello!" came the more astringent, tightly-wound tones of Jim Nicholson. "We're calling for Roger."

"One moment, gentlemen." Putting them on hold, Frances called out to Roger, still staring with concern out the front door: "It's your conference call."

Roger walked quickly in her direction. "I forgot all about it. I was supposed to give some thought to the next picture over the weekend."

"Oh, dear."

He moved past Frances into his office, where he grabbed a sip of coffee and a bite of scrambled egg toast before tapping the speaker button of his telephone. Frances peeked in and saw him seated behind his desk, gesturing for her to join him—just keep quiet—moral support and all that.

"Good morning, gentlemen!" Roger cheered.

"Congratulations, buddy!" Arkoff cried. "When Mantle hits a homer, you know it's gonna stop eventually but when Corman belts one . . . 3.5 million and climbing! Holy Moses!"

Sam's tendency to pour it on thick was one of numerous discomforts Roger was required to endure with his distributor. His insincerity required him to be insincere in turn.

"Thanks, Sam," he said, doing his best to sustain the joviality. "Did you hear I'm being sued by the San Bernardino chapter of the Hell's Angels?"

"What for, for God's sake?"

"Four million dollars. And they've announced they plan to kill me once they collect."

"No, no—I mean, what are they suing you for?"

"Defamation of character," Roger grinned.

Sam could be heard punching the air with a fist of delight. "You can't *buy* publicity like this! Jim, let's get out a press release on this."

"Right away," his partner promised. "You know, Rog, you just might make enough from this picture to pay 'em off. It's my pleasure to inform you that *The Wild Angels* is now on track to become the highest-grossing motion picture in AIP's history."

"Gentlemen, that's most gratifying."

Frances glowed, so pleased for her boss.

"It just goes to show you don't need to work for the majors to have a major career in this town, Roger," Sam observed. "You've rewritten the rule book," he added, in that special way he had of making the God's honest truth sound and smell suspiciously like horse crap. "And we would like to talk to you now about the *next* biggest picture in the history of AIP."

"Okay. . . " Roger allowed, warily.

"This script is bold, Roger. Something new! Something never before seen! In ColorScope!"

Jim added: "You're just the man for it, Rog. How does this title grab you . . . *The Devil's Angels*!"

Roger rolled his eyes and faked a mulling-over pause. "I'm sure it'll do great box office, fellas, but I'm thinking along somewhat different lines."

On their end, Sam and Jim exchanged troubled glances.

"Different?" they responded in unison.

"Frankly, I haven't discussed this with you before because, well, truthfully . . . I'm not certain this project is right for AIP."

Frances eased back into the chair below the "X"—*The Man with the X-Ray Eyes* poster to enjoy the spectacle of her boss in action. Roger shrugged for her edification, making a frantic face to signal the fact that he pretty much had *bupkis*.

"What do you mean?" blurted Jim. "You haven't been talking to another studio, have you, Rog?"

"I don't have to meet with one, Jim—I'm *at* one. I have a three-picture deal here at Columbia and they want me to start handing them over."

"Never bullshit a bullshitter, Roger," Sam interrupted with coarse but almost refreshing sincerity. "I know they're passing on everything you send upstairs over there. Do you think the likes of a Dick Zanuck or a Charlie Bluhdorn is impressed by a guy who can piss out a picture in two days?"

"Hey, Sam," Jim advised *sotto voce*, counseling a cooler head approach. "C'mon."

Silently, vigorously, Frances shook her head: "YES!"

"I'm not putting it down, goddammit! I *respect* it! Y'see, Roger, what you are is a maverick. A fornicating, genu-ine maverick. Now. Do you know what a maverick is?"

"Yes," Roger confirmed, turning on his Stanford graduate authority. "A maverick is a steer that wanders away from the herd to go its own way."

"Right!" Sam approved. "And that is why AIP will *always* be your home!"

"For a few more pictures, at least," Jim added. "Contractually speaking."

"Okay, then," Roger allowed. "Then let me go my own way." He rose from the desk and began to pace around the office.

"Have we ever stopped you?" Sam wailed. "We just wanna *hear* it!"

"Yeah," Jim interjected. "We're all ears, Rog."

At this point, Iris found her way into Roger's world, having somehow navigated her passage from the outer office through the rooms of a crumbling 17th century mansion, the subterranean dungeons and torture devices of a 15th century Spanish *castillo*, the Bronson Caverns headquarters of a Venusian invader, and the farthest reaches of a terrified galaxy. This may explain why she planted her foot on the room's threshold with all the gravity of a tightrope walker returning to terra firma. Talking a deep breath, she held up her handbag.

"Isn't it pretty?" she cheered. "I got it at a boutique in Berkeley called Your Mother's Mustache!"

Roger and Frances stared at her interruption blankly. She had been gone long enough for them to both forget she was there.

Iris looked at their faces. "Oh. Not just now, of course," she explained.

"What's going on there, Roger?" Sam inquired. "I thought this was a private call."

Iris looked up, startled, and turned to Frances. "This office . . . *talks?*"

Roger held a shushing finger to his lips and pointed to Frances' matching chair, silently but emphatically mouthing "Sit Down!" Iris missed the chair and happily sank down onto the floor, where she began stroking the carpet as if petting a cat.

"It's just a friend, Sam." Then Roger carefully drew his partners back into the conversation by tap-dancing out of sheer desperation. "Okay, fellas, let me start here by asking you both a question."

"Shoot," Sam dared him.

Roger stared at the poster for "X"—*The Man with the X-Ray Eyes*, the world-weary eyes of Ray Milland glowering back at him. Inwardly, Roger demanded that the image on the poster give its will over to him. He had no idea what he was about to say, but it came out thusly: "What is . . . reality?"

"Beg pardon?"

"What *is* reality—to you, or Jim, or me?"

"I'm afraid you're losing us, Rog," Jim confessed.

"Now . . . just bear with me a moment, fellas. Let's look hard at that question."

"This is a story about . . . a professional man . . . say . . . a director. Not a film director, but . . . let's say a man who directs television commercials . . ."

"Sounds like an old guy, Roger," Sam fretted.

"Peter Fonda," Roger reassured him. "I'm thinking Peter."

"Go on."

"He's young, but he's trapped. Burnt out. Successful, but—you know—is that enough? He's got women, cars, money . . . but something is missing."

Frances thought to herself, *He's got that right.*

Sam cut in. "Why don't we save this one for Fellini?"

"Hang on, Sam," Jim cut in, helpfully. "What happens, Rog?"

The X poster had given Roger as much as it was going to, so he turned and saw the stack of magazines still sitting there beside his trusty caliper. At the top of the stack was the issue of *Newsweek* with its LSD cover story.

Roger clamped his eyes shut. "He takes a drug," he continued, suddenly opening his eyes widely, feeling as certain as he had ever been certain about anything in his life. He turned back to the X poster, remembering what Etienne Lipschitz the French critic had said about the film. "He takes a drug to see through the layers of reality." Then he looked at Frances, grinning from ear to ear. "He takes a drug that transforms the way he sees and feels."

The ensuing silence was suddenly split by a sound that seemed remarkably akin to a yahoo.

"An LSD movie!" Sam squealed. "The kids'll love it! Damn it, Jim—let's not waste any time. Let's do it now—before the kids start getting high on something else!"

"Ready when you are, Sam," Roger smiled, sinking back into his office chair with victorious relief.

"Say, Rog," Jim asked, "who's writing the script? Is it in hand? We might have time to make our Christmas release schedule."

Roger had not thought that far ahead, obviously, but Frances—rocking in her chair like a fan in the bleachers at the Super Bowl—mouthed "Chuck."

"Chuck!" he nearly shouted in recognition. "Chuck Griffith is doing it."

"Who?"

"Our *Wild Angels* man," Roger boasted. "It's not in hand yet, but no matter. I don't really see this as a Christmas picture."

"Christmas shmistmas," Sam reprimanded his partner, before turning his error into lavish praise. "This has 'Big Summer Release' written all over it!"

"Then we're off to the races," agreed Jim. "I'll get the art department cracking on some poster ideas."

This was the way things were done at AIP: Before a script was even written, when the ink on the idea was still wet, they had their guys in the art department—Albert Kallis or Reynold Brown—create a poster, which they then took to film industry conventions and pre-sold and pre-booked. Then, and only then, was a script actually commissioned—but, in this case, the horse was as good as out of the gate. This was the next film from the director of *The Wild Angels*, for Chrissakes.

Sam was feeling his exploitation oats. "Wait a minute, do we have a title yet for this magnum-o-poose?"

Roger studied his girlfriend closely. Iris was looking up at the framed posters and awards on walls with the expression of a marionette caught in its own strings. Her expression was poetic, haunting, distant.

"We'll call it *The Trip*, Sam," Roger decided. "Thank you, gentlemen. To Be Continued."

He punched out, ending the call on a high note.

Roger's joyful expression then dropped like a mask, revealing a second visage of great seriousness beneath.

"And this young lady needs to take one," he said, pointing to Marsha. "Call her a taxi, Frances. We have work to do!"

Less than 10 minutes later, Iris was hanging out the back window of a Yellow Cab, waving a giddy goodbye to Frances. She had to promise her it was the Yellow Submarine before she would get inside.

When she came back inside the office, Frances found Roger's door closed.

On the other side of this present barricade, Roger was sitting behind his desk, doing his best to marshal and collect his thoughts. Initially, his thoughts were of Iris—the spacey, lost woman-child; then his thoughts retreated further back to Robin, the waitressing film student so ardent in the ways of Ingmar Bergman; but then the sight of the caliper paperweight on his desk shifted his thoughts in another, still more retrospective direction—back to 1964. June, he supposed.

Seated in the chair across from him was one of several young women he had interviewed on that particular day for the position of Personal Assistant. She had just graduated from college and had been sent to him as a graduate job referral. She was attractive, young, and auburn-haired; beyond that, an intriguing combination of the confident and the vulnerable. But what most caused her to stand out in Roger's memory—or so he thought—was that she came in not really wanting the job.

Roger remembered looking over the questionnaire she had filled out: name (Julie Ann Halloran), place of birth (Omaha, Nebraska), educational background, special interests...

"Thank you for coming in, Miss Halloran," he said. "I see you were sent here on job referral from UCLA. Have you also applied for other jobs?"

"Yes, there were two others. One was for a position in marketing at the *L.A. Times*—that was, well... never mind, and the other was at an advertising agency."

"What were you going to say?"

"Really? Okay, I was going to say that is the one I'm most hoping for. Not that I wouldn't love working here, I'm sure!"

"Working in marketing, that's your dream job?"

"No, but working in marketing might put me in proximity to my dream job."

"Which is?" he smiled.

"To be one of those people down in the newspaper morgue who do research."

Roger's brows seemed to clamp down on the idea.

"My idea of a good time," she continued, "is having all the time and resources in the world to research anything and everything I want to know more about."

"That could prove useful here, as well. Research is definitely in the purview of the position. What's something else about you?"

"I like to solve problems," she added. "You know, making things work."

"I see," Roger saw.

"I'm guessing you do, too," she ventured.

"Why do you say that?"

"Well, I've heard you once made a movie in two days. Is that true?"

Roger nodded affirmatively.

"Some people might say it was reckless," Julie observed. "But I would say something like that takes considerable planning!"

"And you'd be right," Roger confirmed.

"I know the type. I am the type. Two of my uncles are engineers."

"Really? I majored in engineering at Stanford."

His comment made her giggle. She explained herself: "Isn't that the sort of thing I should be telling you?"

"Well," Roger grinned, "this is all good. You're curious, resourceful—*and* a strategic thinker." Then his grin burst its hinges as he added, "And, if you worked here, as you've seen from our poster displays out there, it's kind of like working in a morgue!"

They laughed.

"Do you like horror pictures?" Roger asked.

Julie shrank in her seat. "Anything *but* horror movies, actually," she said. "I saw *Samson and Delilah* when I was little, and when they blinded Victor Mature, I had nightmares for weeks. Then I saw *The Day the Earth Stood Still* and... *brrrrr!* That's when I decided I did *not* like to be scared at the movies."

"Do you have a favorite movie?"

"Oh, no question! *Francis the Talking Mule*."

"Look," he said, "Julie—if I may—I'll be absolutely frank with you. I can't offer you the job. Earlier today, another applicant for the job came in here with an Oxford diploma."

"Is that what she said," Julie smiled. "An Oxford *diploma*?"

Roger smiled back. (How many other applicants would have caught this?) "Pardon me," he interjected, grinning back. "An Oxford *degree*. Anyway, she's won awards for short films she's made, she's knowledgeable about the work I've done, and her voice is going to sound great on the phone when people call the office. I can't *not* hire her."

"I see."

"That said... I'm enjoying our conversation, and I wonder if I might interest you in continuing it... over *dinner*?"

It happens that Julie was so inclined; they had dinner together, they liked one another, and they became good friends. Neither of them thought of their relationship as romantic. Julie had a steady boyfriend since college and, whenever the two of them joined Roger for dinner, he usually had a new companion on his arm to introduce.

When Roger first began toying with the idea of making *The Wild Angels*, he prevailed upon his connection with Julie to call her over at the

Times, where by then she had become happily employed—after an equally happy spell at the ad agency. He asked, knowing the pleasure she took in research, if she might research a community of motorcycle enthusiasts calling themselves "Hell's Angels." He was planning to make a picture about them. She agreed and, after doing what she had agreed to do, she called him back to say, "Roger, whatever you do, *don't have anything to do with them!*"

Aside from the lawsuit, it's a good thing he didn't listen to her.

Roger blinked, now back from his involuntary reverie. He opened the *Newsweek* magazine in front of him and started jotting down some notes on a pad. Almost as a reflex, he reached for the telephone to call Julie. It had been a while since they'd talked. But somehow, he felt that she might even be more concerned about his current subject matter.

Instead, he buzzed Frances.

Somewhat exhausted from the Iris adventure but determined not to show it, she knocked on the door and swung it open. To see him sitting there, already moving forward on a project conceived out of sheer desperation, so serious, so industrious, so impressive—there wasn't much she wouldn't forgive him. "You rang?"

Without looking up, without so much as a break in his scribbling, Roger asked, "Frances, do you know anything about L...S...D...? I mean, personally?"

"Why not ask your friend Iris? She seemed well versed with the subject."

There was a measured pause.

"Be that as it may," he resumed, ripping the page from his notepad and slapping it on the desk. "Sam and Jim have an opening date, so I had better start studying up on L...S...D. I need to know more about my subject—from both popular and academic perspectives. I want you to get me everything you can on the subject of L...S...D. Huxley, Watts, Leary. Oh yes, and this *Tibetan Book of the Dead*."

"You usually turn to Julie for research, don't you?"

"Not this time," he said. "She might...not approve." He was also concerned that she might worry, or even reconsider their friendship in light of his attraction to unstable subject matter. *Was this what attracted him? Instability?*

Frances took the sheet from his desk, giving it the once-over. "Alright then," she said. "Which card shall I put these on?"

Roger fished the wallet from his hip pocket and handed her a card, saying "Here, this should cover it."

She looked at her hand in dismay. "Your library card!? How about a bus pass?"

The next thing Roger had to do was secure his screenwriter. This involved driving out to Venice Beach, home to veteran (and affordable) scenarist Charles B. Griffith.

It was late afternoon—early morning for Chuck—when Roger found himself in the beatnik scribe's apartment, which was not unlike Roger's concept of an opium den. As Chuck made industrious noises on the other side of a green-and-white beaded curtain covering the ingress to his kitchenette, Roger tried to make himself comfortable in a new-fangled piece of furniture called a beanbag chair. On the turntable, crackling from heavy use, was "Giant Steps" by John Coltrane.

He looked from side to side, taking note of all the little thingamajigs unearthed by Chuck over years of nesting. There were tiny Buddhas, Grove Press paperbacks, a smoking joss stick, a dream catcher, haphazard arrangements of record albums (many on the Impulse! label), a Royal manual typewriter, and stacks of loose typed pages anchored aground by various conch shells. Roger felt certain from all this detritus that Chuck was indeed the right man for this assignment.

Chuck, dressed in an Oriental bathrobe and cut-off jeans, with a cigarette hanging from his lip, was rustling up some breakfast. "Sure you don't want any?" he called out, over the considerable volume of his percolator. "My *huevos rancheros* are deservedly legendary, if I do say so myself."

"No, thanks," Roger answered, waving away a persistent noodling of incense smoke. "Chuck, there *is* a point to my visit."

"I figured," Chuck said. "Otherwise, you'd summon me to your office. I figured you must be in a jam and need something P.D.Q. Hang on a sec."

With epicurean flair, he poured his Kona coffee, tossed a shot of Hennessey into it, and plopped down into the matching beanbag opposite Roger. "Shoot," he said, shoveling a fork load of spicy eggs into his mouth.

"Chuck, you know something about drugs, don't you?"

The wordsmith looked at his old colleague with a twinkle of bemusement. "I may kiss but I never tell."

"Now, I'm not talking about marijuana. You were, of course, very helpful to me on *The Wild Angels*, knowing how to obtain those creature comforts we were asked to procure for our, our technical advisors. In this case, I am talking about recreational pharmaceuticals."

"Why do you ask?"

"Because—assuming it's not foreign ground to you—I would like to interest you in writing a screenplay on the subject of today's drug culture. Specifically, L . . . S . . . D."

"Acid."

"Acid?"

"Yeah," Chuck explained. "Nobody calls it LSD anymore. Except maybe narcs and PTA members."

"Good to know."

"Really, Roger? An *acid* movie? Far out." He took a swig of his coffee, savoring the thought.

Roger could see he was intrigued.

"Any guidelines," Chuck then asked, "or do you just want me to do my usual thing and suffer the consequences?"

"I don't know what you mean."

"C'mon, Rog! You know how it's been lately. I do the first draft, then you get some asshole to rewrite me for the big paycheck."

"Chuck, I can assure you that *no one* is getting the big paycheck."

Then Chuck got "that look," the one that Roger likened intellectually to a mud turtle, hunkering down into some deep, primordial stubbornness. He continued to eat in stony silence, his rigid disposition gradually relaxed by the emollients of a cleaned plate and a drained mug.

"Sorry, man," he said, "I was digging Trane's solo. So. When do you need this masterpiece?"

"Two weeks."

"Give me a logline."

"Couldn't you just . . . "

"No, we've tried that. Don't make me guess. What's the story *you* want to tell?"

Roger took the better part of a minute to formulate his answer. "A man is unhappy," he said.

"And rain is wet," Chuck snorted. "Anything else?"

"Just give me the Secret of the Universe in 85 pages."

"I can do that."

CHAPTER 7

September 1966

ROGER HAZARDED A GUESS: "New telephone books?"

Frances had just burst into his office, carrying—as best she could—a large and rather unwieldy cardboard box. She dropped the parcel on his desk. "Judging by the return address... this is either the head of Peter Bogdanovich, or Chuck's script!"

Roger tore into the package. Inside the box were flats of cardboard, beneath which he fought through a froth of excelsior. Beneath this was a capacious swath of tightly-taped bubble wrap, which gave way to a layers of tissue paper wound (with a stoner's determination) around a mailing envelope containing a proud, deluxe, leatherette binder. By the time he reached it, Roger felt as though he'd performed a Caesarian section on a dolphin in order to perform lung surgery on its fetus. His eyes popped when he glimpsed the number 539 in the upper right corner of the last of its pages.

Roger flashed back to Chuck's script for their 1958 film *The Undead*, which was based on one of AIP's poster schemes. The only note he had given to Chuck was that poster—a real beauty, showing a living skeleton, heralded by bats, raising the folds of its cloak to reveal a lovely young woman in a Baby Doll negligée framed by a coffin. When Chuck's script finally arrived, Roger's back was so near the wall that he had no choice but to go ahead and film it as it was, even though he had turned in a tale of witchcraft set in the Middle Ages with all the dialogue in iambic pentameter.

The Trip!—the unsolicited exclamation point suggested a musical along the lines of *Oklahoma!* or *Hello Dolly!*—did indeed deliver on the dreaded promise of various musical numbers, not to mention an Intermission and an Entr'acte. The first word on the first page was "Overture," followed by an introductory invocation to be spoken by Bruce Dern (in a kind of *oltretomba* form of his late *Wild Angels* character, Loser)—in subtitled Latin, no less.

"He's got to be kidding!" Roger finally said. "It'll take me longer to read it than it took him to write it!"

"Longer than it took you to open it," noted Frances.

"He'll have to chop this thing down."

Frances made an apologetic, *tsk*ing sound. "Roger, you forget, our friend the author is presently out of the country for two weeks. His annual sabbatical to Peru."

"Great, just great," he griped, throwing everything back into the box. "I need to find someone who can do a rewrite—and fast! Who do we know?"

The question hung in the air, no ready answer forthcoming.

Roger headed for the door, staggering under the box in his arms.

"Wait," Frances called out, "where are you going?"

"I'll be at home. Reading."

"You're going to read it?"

"I paid for it. Who knows, there might be something useful in it."

"You can't read here?"

"Yes, but I can also *drink* at home."

In a driveway outside the Santa Monica home of sometimes actress Sandra Knight, a 1958 Karmann Ghia was on the receiving end of some cheap repair by two fellow actors: John Hackett and her soon-to-be *ex*-husband, Jack Nicholson. It was Jack's car, bought used once upon a time. Now limned with rust and corrosion, it had seen better days. He had been at Sandy's to pick up some mail—no residuals, just bills—when the thing just up and died.

John, Jack and Sandra had been friends since the 1950s, when they were all students in Martin Landau's acting class. It was from there they made the joint decision to advance into Jeff Corey's workshop—and there that they met Roger Corman. Roger's interest in acting was never quite the equal of theirs—acting was never his air and water, his bread and butter—yet it was his serene, serendipitous presence that would make their respective fortunes, such as they were. Roger had been impressed by Jack's talent, but what tempted him over to talk with him after class was his outgoing, madcap personality—people just plain liked "the Irishman," a nickname he'd given himself. Subsequently, Roger cast Jack in pretty much every movie he presently had under his belt—*The Cry Baby Killer, The Little Shop of Horrors* and *The Wild Ride*; on one occasion, he even hired him to pose in imaginary scenes for the stills, posters and lobby cards used for *The T-Bird Gang,* an independently-made pick-up in which Jack didn't even appear but which had no visual charm of its own. Jack had also been cast as Peter Lorre's disappointingly bland son in *The Raven* (a disappointingly bland part) and subsequently played opposite Sandy as the romantic leads in a patchwork production called *The Terror,* which ended-up being co-directed by almost everyone Roger had ever taken under his wing.

Hackett was part of all this, too. He had played a French policeman in the "Black Cat" segment of Roger's *Tales of Terror* before getting cast in a couple of Corman-produced movies directed by *Wild Angels* editor Monte Hellman, which Jack had happened to star in and write—not that anybody ever saw them. At least they got some memories of dysentery to draw on, in case a future role ever demanded it.

Sandy, who cared less about acting than either of them, could lay claim to having the most recent paycheck for treading the boards. As a favor to Stephanie Rothman, an award-winning film student who at the time was occupying the third office in Roger's suite, she had agreed to act in some scenes being added to *Operation Titian,* a Yugoslavian picture Roger had been unable to sell. For a few hectic days' work, she'd earned enough to buy a few pizzas. The result was currently playing in drive-ins coast to coast as *Blood Bath*—"starring" Sandra Knight. Such was life.

"Hand me that wrench, willya?" Hackett said to Jack, who sat sullenly awaiting instruction behind the steering column. Hackett, the one who actually knew something about fixing cars, was under the hood—which, in this instance, happened to be in the boot of the crazy, ass-backwards vehicle.

Jack got out, carrying the wrench back to Hackett like it weighed 50 pounds.

"So, long story short," Hackett concluded, summarizing the current state of his next best bet in picture business, "Derns was telling me we might get the whole thing financed on my lawyer's credit card."

"Sounds good," Jack grumbled. "Just remember your old pal, when it gets up and running. Like this goddamn car."

Hackett finished doing whatever he was doing under the hood, then told Jack, "Okay now, hit it." He sure as hell wanted to; the damn thing never worked. A few moments later, with Jack turning the key and revving the motor, the car was making a terrible howling noise, which then sputtered, settling into a more grating noise that choked to slow death.

Jack killed the ignition, tired and hot and disgusted.

Hackett was suddenly standing beside him. "Sorry, *amigo*. Looks like it's back to the shop for this old buggy."

"Fuck me," he spat, striking the wheel with the butt of his hand. "That's another two hundred bucks I don't have."

Hackett was able to take him as far as Westwood in his Rambler; from there, Jack was able to hitch as far as Sunset and Rodeo—where nobody feels self-conscious for standing on the curb, covered with axle grease with their thumb out. He was coming to the conclusion that the prospects for a lift were probably not too swell when a Porsche that nearly passed him suddenly halted and sounded its horn. Jack blessed the Angels and trotted after it, where he discovered Roger Corman—of all people—behind the wheel, looking on top of the world, as always.

"Jack! Hop in. Where are you headed?"

Jack stood outside the door, uncertain, half-afraid to even touch the car door. "Are you sure? I'm headed toward Melrose."

The horns of cars queued behind Roger were honking. "Me, too," he said for the sake of argument.

"Peachy," Jack said, climbing in and settling himself lightly so as not to mar the upholstery.

Roger resumed driving. Jack noticed the Herb Alpert 8-track lodged in the tape deck—"Tijuana Taxi" was playing, appropriately enough.

"Car in the shop?" Roger inquired.

"That's about the size of it. How the hell you doin', man? Been awhile."

"Never better. *The Wild Angels* is a big hit."

"Glad to hear it," Jack responded, dully. He would have loved to have a piece of that. But no, he'd been in the Philippines with Monte and a permanently upset stomach.

Roger noticed that his old friend's mood was overcast. "Jack, is something wrong?"

Jack owed a great deal to Roger, and he struggled visibly with whether or not to answer candidly. Then, to his own surprise, before he could even consider the alternative, the words started pouring out of him like the java at Barney's Beanery, hot and bitter.

"Roger, I'm 30 years old and I work harder at this business than anyone else I know and there ain't a goddamn soul in this mother-lovin' town that wants to hire me as an actor. Every movie I've ever been in just fell off the planet... and the ones I wrote, they crapped out just as bad." He fell silent; he was close to sobbing. "You're the only guy in town who's ever—*ever*—given me real, honest-to-goodness work and I'm grateful—hand-to-heart, I am—but... well, let's just say *The Terror* didn't exactly put me on the map..." Thinking back to those days when he was sitting on horseback in uniform on the coastline at the Leo Carrillo Beach in Malibu, trying to sell himself as Lt. Andre Duvalier (late of Napoleon's Army), he didn't know whether to weep or to laugh.

"Jack," Roger said firmly, having no time for all this. "What do you know about L... S... D? Acid, I mean."

Jack stopped short and looked at Roger with weird, unexpected, out-of-left-field amusement.

"Did you just say 'Acid'?"

"Yes. I assume you've partaken?"

"I have," Jack confessed. "Personally, I dig it, but I don't know what that says about me. A shrink gave some to me and Sandy for our marriage counseling. We're splitting up, in case ya haven't heard."

"That's too bad," Roger offered. "I've always liked Sandy. She was very good, I thought, in *Frankenstein's Daughter*—an otherwise undistinguished effort."

"Yeah, well, Frankenstein's Daughter didn't cotton too well to LSD therapy. She looked at me while I was re-experiencing my own birth and thought I was some kind of a demon."

"Interesting," Roger judged. "Ever consider writing a movie about it?"

"A movie? About acid?"

"Chuck Griffith gave me some pages," he understated, "but I don't know... I think I need something more... more..."

"Violent?" Jack hazarded a guess. "Gory? Edgar Allan Poey?"

"Not necessarily. Actually, no... more *real*. You see, I'm moving in a more *real* direction. A prominent French critic pointed this out to me recently. People everywhere are becoming curious about this substance. I want to explore it, really study it from all angles. I want to make a picture that will depict what it's like to take 'a trip'—as they call it—and come out the other end." He looked over at Jack. "Interested?"

Jack cocked an eyebrow. "Hell, yeah!" he grinned. "I mean, we gotta be talkin' about at least a couple hundred dollars, right?"

A half-block further on, he repeated: "Right?"

Roger drove Jack back to Harry Dean's place. He was somewhat taken aback when Roger opened the trunk of his car and hoisted out a box that looked like it might have contained the body of a small Chicago gangster. "Here," Jack offered, "let me give ya a hand."

Jack carried the box inside while chattering amiably about Harry's recent good fortune, getting gigs in TV Westerns and such. He showed Roger to the kitchen, where he gave him a choice of water or apple juice.

"Apple juice," Roger said. "I'm starving."

Jack smiled, taking a mental note of the line as he poured the juice into two small glasses and popped the carton back into the refrigerator. "Tasty!" he said, after draining his—and then his demeanor turned serious and considerate. "Roger, I know your time is valuable but I want to give you my fullest attention. So, I'm gonna put on a record and then I'm gonna go wash up. The music will help pass the time. I promise I won't be gone more than one or two songs."

"Alright."

Jack disappeared into the next room, and Roger heard some hushed preparatory sounds before the phonograph stylus was heard sinking and locking into a turning vinyl groove. In those next five minutes, Roger poked around the house—he saw a Royal manual typewriter, a compact reel-to-reel recorder, a shelf with bottles of tequila and mescal, a worn acoustic guitar with a beaded strap—while absorbing the first two tracks from the new Beach Boys album, *Pet Sounds*.

The first song he had heard second-hand around town, on other car radios and such; it was upbeat and a little melancholy, wistful. He liked it. As it rose to its extended fade-out, he could picture cheerleaders singing it while rustling their pom-poms. However, the next song was unexpectedly candid, intimate and transporting. As it continued playing, he took a seat on a handy chair to listen more attentively. The words to "You Still Believe In Me" could be applied to any number of different relationships, but under these circumstances, they caused Roger to reflect on the duration of his friendship with Jack, how their careers seemed to drift apart but always came back together. After that, the next song had an impulsive, momentous sound that made him want to get in his car and drive somewhere, not to go anywhere specifically but rather to think things through, to sort something out. *Maybe I shouldn't be listening to so much instrumental music*, he was thinking as Jack rushed back downstairs, wearing a clean white T-shirt and jeans. He was barefoot and smiling like a wild card.

"Sorry I kept ya waiting," Jack said. He showed Roger into what would have been the dining room, if Harry Dean had sunk any dough in dining room furniture. As it was, there was a chest of drawers, two wooden chairs tucked into opposing corners, an apple crate bookshelf, and some Fillmore posters on the wall, but it was mostly a large open floor covered by a cheap but not unattractive Persian rug.

"Harry calls this here his conversation pit," Jack said, turning the record down to background levels and inviting Roger to sit on the floor. He carried the box into the room and dropped it on the floor with a thump.

Soon pages of Chuck Griffith's *magnum opus* were spread everywhere, each Act, each song in its own stack. Roger smiled as Jack methodically picked out the hundred or so pages of lyrical content and moved them off to the side, where they wouldn't obscure a clear view of all the rest. He could see that Jack was taking this work seriously, that he proceeded diligently. He appreciated the care he was taking.

"It looks real interesting, Roger, it does," Jack finally said, "but would you, like . . . mind if I just . . . you know . . . started over from scratch?"

"Would that yield quicker results?"

Jack turned contemplative and raised an index finger. Without uncrossing his legs, he stood up and moved across the room to a chest of drawers. From the uppermost drawer, he produced a stash box and pulled out a joint pre-wrapped in yellow paper.

He came back, stood in front of Roger, re-crossed his legs, and then dropped back down opposite him. He moistened the joint between his lips, lit it up with a magically produced Pez-shaped lighter, and took a deep hit.

Roger watched with fascination.

"Well," he estimated with his breath deeply held, "quicker than getting bogged-down in a lot of . . . hedge trimming, if you know what I mean." He blew the aromatic smoke toward the ceiling.

"I see."

"And if we did go that way, it's just possible we might find there are no trees *without* the forest—if you know what I'm sayin'."

Roger paused, seeming to ponder this point. "Jack," he finally said, "Jack, is that a marijuana cigarette that you're smoking?"

Jack took a good long look at the burning stick in his hand. "Roger, what I've got here is, in fact, a reefer. You mean to say you've never . . . ?"

"I've been around it. I had to make a deal with the Hell's Angels on this last picture: their cooperation in exchange for four cases of Budweiser and a kilo of . . . Tijuana Gold, I think they called it."

"*Acapulco* Gold, Rog—*Acapulco*," Jack corrected him. "Hold the phone! You scored 'em a kilo of the most primo of prime grass and you didn't even *try* it?"

"I was working."

"Well, you're not workin' now."

With a raised eyebrow, Jack held the joint out to Roger. He took it between pinching fingers and looked down the length of it as though it were an alien artifact.

Jack finally got the drop on the fact that they had now listened to Side 1 of *Pet Sounds* a few times in a row—not that he was ready to get up and do anything about it. He and Roger were more into noticing how some of the patterns in the weave of the Persian rug floated on higher and lower levels than others when Roger, still red-faced from a previous laugh, suddenly began giggling again like a schoolboy.

Jack was intrigued. "What's so funny, man?"

"Do you promise not to laugh?"

"No."

"I feel like a Beatle."

This idea got Jack laughing too. "You *are* the fuckin' Beatles, man!" he realized.

This made Roger laugh even harder.

Jack finally got off his ass to deal with the record player. From the next room, he called out, "Hey, you know, Peter—your movie star—he took acid with the Beatles."

Roger exhaled the smoke he'd been holding in his lungs. "Peter... *Bogdanovich?*"

"Peter *Fonda*. For real, man. I heard the event took place in Zsa Zsa Gabor's bathroom. That musta been a trip in itself. You know the Beatles song 'She Said, She Said'? It was written about him."

"It's called '*She* Said' and it's about *him*?" Roger regarded the smoke in the roach in the roach clip in his hand. "I think this marijuana may be having an effect."

"You think so?" Jack held his inquisitive expression until it exploded in new laughter.

"Say, Jack," Roger said as he passed the joint back approvingly, "would you know where I might obtain more of this?"

"It'll cost ya," Jack teased.

Roger's brow furrowed. "I've always heard that the first one is always free."

"That *was* your first one," Jack pointed out.

"Never mind."

That night, as the sound of a police siren passed by the house in stereo, Jack Nicholson sat staring at the blank page in his typewriter, trying to imagine what it would be like to turn the key in a fully-repaired Karmann-Ghia. He had been in dry dock since he had taken the chair, the snow-like whiteness of the paper blazing back into his eyes. Then he suddenly remembered the old adage that ink begets ink, that the best way to make the words flow is to get some words, any words, onto the paper—so he began to type.

He stopped to regard the sentence he had written: *All work and no play makes Jack a dull boy.*

No, that wasn't ever going to lead him anywhere.

Frowning, he stood up and shook his limp arms, then ran in place furiously for several seconds to get his blood flowing. Method acting 101. He reached behind the typewriter and turned on a portable Zenith AM/FM radio. A slow turn of the dial turned up a news report *("The Pentagon released the figures for American casualties for the week of September...")*, "My World Is Empty Without You" by The Supremes, Sgt. Barry Sadler's "The Ballad Of The Green Berets," a smooth-voiced DJ acknowledging a just-concluded song by The Modern Jazz Quartet, Tammy Wynette's "D-I-V-O-R-C-E," and "Take A Giant Step" by The Monkees. That's where the roulette ball settled, on The Monkees—hell, it would be a different song in two minutes or less, anyway—and he fired up a little stub of hash.

By the time the station got around to playing "Open My Eyes" by The Nazz, Jack was typing like he was taking dictation from another place. As The Nazz faded into "Gloria" by Shadows of Knight, he opened his eyes and re-read what had just flowed out of him.

His protagonist was named Paul Groves. Why Paul Groves? Maybe it came from hearing Paul McCartney sing "Drive My Car" on the radio playlist and the fact that he was currently reading Frantz Fanon's *The Wretched of the Earth*, published by Grove Press. Anyway, this Paul Groves was a disenchanted director of television commercials for products with names like April In Paris and Adventures In Paradise (AIP, get it?) who was separated from a wife, Sally, whom he still loved, in anticipation of divorce. (Was Sally too similar to Sandy? Fuck it, like anyone knew or cared about their business.)

Through a group of friends, like he had met up again with Roger, Paul makes the acquaintance of John (Beatles reference), a straight but illuminated cat who agrees to serve as his guide on his first-ever acid trip. They score the acid from a dealer named Max (a part with Hopper written all over it), he drops it and he grooves. He even used the apple juice line that Roger gave him. Now all he needed was the Secret of the Universe part.

It would come. He knew it would come.

Pleased with this achievement, and the fact that he was already on Page 15, Jack leaped to his feet and danced around the room to the jangling music.

He was on a roll.

A wallop of thunder and lightning caused the light levels on the matte painting (gothic castle, low angle) to flicker. While looking at this opening reel again in the editing room, Roger estimated this was probably the fifth or sixth time he had made use of this impressive shot, which Albert Whitlock himself—the best matte painter in the business, under contract to Universal—had knocked off for some under-the-table pay while on vacation. However, it was an expense he hadn't intended, so it became a problem. Roger then solved the problem by selling off the footage to a stock footage company for relicensing. Years after its original commission, it continued to pop up in television episodes set in haunted castles, Halloween season commercials, and even features cobbled together by the Competition.

This *faux* exterior shot then cut to Boris Karloff prowling the hallways of a dank castle—in fact, leftover sets from *The Raven*. Karloff himself was something like a leftover set from *The Raven*. New product slapped together from free leftovers and it looked like a million bucks, even on the small Steenbeck editing screen. Roger's attitude toward the footage was one of pride, but he had obtained infinitely more satisfaction from conceiving the plan for making a new feature out of virtually nothing than from actually watching it. It was the difference between solving a problem (which held great interest) and watching a solved problem (which, of course, was unnecessary).

Peter Bogdanovich, on the other hand—who was seated beside him—actually took pleasure from the product. Go figure.

Now Jack Nicholson, dressed as a soldier from the Napoleonic wars, was knocking on Karloff's door. It was Roger's accidental meeting with Jack the other day that dropped the penny on this new idea that was riding him.

"Peter," Roger said at the psychological moment, "you may recall this picture I made a few years ago . . . *The Terror*."

Bogdanovich, not knowing why he had been summoned, lapsed effortlessly into his Karloff impression: "What you thee, Leftenant, are the remainth of a noble houth . . . "

Roger looked back at him blankly, having long since forgotten the line.

"I know the movie, Roger," the younger man clarified in his own voice. "Boris Karloff is a crazy Baron and Jack Nicholson is a French soldier in tights."

Roger flicked off the Steenbeck. "So, what do you think?"

"Tights are not a good look for Jack Nicholson. What does this have to do with your LSD movie?"

"Nothing," Roger assured him. "I happened to bump into Jack the other day and he mentioned this old project of ours in passing. It jogged my memory and it suddenly clicked with me that we wrapped this film two days ahead of schedule."

"Congratulations."

"You're missing the point."

"Sorry."

"To put it simply: he's not going to like being reminded, but Boris still owes me two days' work." He turned off the Steenbeck's motor and rose abruptly. "Come on, walk with me."

Roger sprang up and the two men started heading back, through connecting corridors, to his office.

"I gave it some thought and realized that, if I were to make use of those two days from Boris for the filming of new material, that could somehow interact with perhaps 15 minutes from *The Terror*—which, believe me, almost no one has seen—a completely new film might be manufactured for as little as $130,000."

"In other words," Bogdanovich mused, "by making this proposed piecemeal picture, you would be spending $120,000 less than your usual budget for a color picture with a star of Karloff's caliber. Which is less than half the current going rate."

"Correct. *And* I would be securing the film's box office guarantee at literally no cost whatsoever."

Peter couldn't help laughing at the sheer audacity of the idea. "Roger—from an artistic standpoint, the idea is frankly appalling. But at the same time, it's kind of irresistible."

"I can't afford *not* to do it," Roger explained. "As for how appalling it may or may not be, I leave that entirely in your hands."

"I don't understand."

"I want *you* to direct this Karloff picture," Roger explained, as he continued walking. He gained about 10 feet of distance before the struck-dumb Bogdanovich realized what had been dropped in his lap. Roger noticed he was walking alone and came back.

"I have a lot on my plate right now, but we can work out the details later. You're interested?"

By the time they had found their way back to Roger's reception area, Bogdanovich was thinking out loud: "So I'll need to come up with a story that somehow incorporates 15 minutes of *The Terror* and two days of Mr. Karloff's time. Sounds like a short picture."

Frances, handling correspondence nearby, smiled at what she was overhearing—having been informed of Roger's scheme earlier that morning. She looked up from her work and let herself be heard: "And perhaps the beginning of a long career?"

It was only then that Bogdanovich absorbed the full gravity of the invitation he had received—no, *the gift* he was being given. This was not only a creative challenge but a tremendous professional opportunity—one others would kill for—and, on top of all that, boy howdy, he would be launching his directorial career with Boris Karloff!

"Thank you, Roger," he said, hoping these words conveyed his deep appreciation. "Count me in."

Roger smiled and they shook hands on it. Frances beamed from the sideline. It was not the first time she had been witness to Roger giving someone a similar opportunity, but the gratitude of those who were shown his favor always made it feel like the first time.

Peter couldn't quite believe his good fortune and began to babble. "I've got to figure out how the hell I'm going to approach this," he said, somewhat dazed. He pictured himself on a set, with Karloff, as his director. How would he proceed? "John Ford, for example, liked to improvise, keep things loose. Hitchcock, on the other hand, storyboarded everything, leaving absolutely nothing to chance."

"You'll be playing with my money on this picture," Roger reminded him. "Think Hitchcock."

Roger and Frances—along with Peter Bogdanovich—had parked on Yucca Street and were now trudging up N. Cherokee to Hollywood Boulevard, their triumvirate in high spirits and looking forward to a celebratory meal at the Musso and Frank Grill. Bogdanovich had called his wife Polly from the office, asking her to meet them there.

"Of course, everyone thinks of Karloff as the Monster," Bogdanovich was saying, "but did you ever see *Scarface*?"

"What's that," Frances joked, "another monster picture?" He knew she was joking.

"Howard Hawks, 1932 . . ." he began to expound, but Frances cut him off with a sudden, hushed, but nonetheless urgent . . .

"Oh, no!"

Bogdanovich saw the *Reagan For Governor* poster stapled to a nearby telephone pole. "Oh, those. Yeah, it's hard to believe, but they're all over town now."

"No, over there!"

Both Roger and Bogdanovich followed the line of her pointing finger to a mixed group of hippie teens in the distance—male, female, black, white—who were taking minimal cover in an alleyway between buildings and passing a joint around.

What had caused Frances to exclaim was the sight of two uniformed LAPD patrolmen, walking purposefully toward this alley, one of them reaching for his nightstick. The other officer got there first, yanking a black kid in a fringed jacket out into the open. He barely had time to flick a lit joint from his hand. The kid struggled, and as soon as he freed himself from the cop's grip, he dropped the evidence and began to hightail it out of there. The cop wielding the nightstick gave chase.

A female in the group—no more than 15, wearing an Indian headband and leather miniskirt, braless under a *Freak Out!* T-shirt—shouted "Leave him alone! He wasn't bothering anybody!"

Everyone watched in horror as the cop in pursuit overtook the fugitive, slamming the truncheon into his legs. The kid shrieked in pain and folded to the pavement.

The girl screamed—yet, despite her fear, she alone rallied to her friend's defense. As she ran toward the fracas to intervene, the other cop tackled her, taking advantage of their tussle to cop a feel in the line of duty. The few others seized the opportunity to race out the opposite end of the alley onto Hollywood Boulevard.

"No, God," Frances said, under her breath.

"This is unacceptable," Roger said firmly, preparing to intervene himself.

"*Don't,* Roger," Frances pleaded. "You'll only make it worse." He seemed to understand and agree.

The three of them stood firm and watched, helplessly. The kid in fringed jacket tried his best to defend himself, crying and yelling while doing so. The cop raised his truncheon once more. There was a bad *whump* as the kid fell silent.

In the end, the girl was let off with a stern warning; after all, the cop got what he wanted and knew she wasn't carrying. As the other officer marched the black kid back to his patrol car, the three accidental witnesses stood shaken and aghast.

"Now *there* goes a dangerous guy."

Roger objected: "Oh, Peter. He did everything he could to avoid having to retaliate."

"I mean *now* he's a dangerous guy," Bogdanovich explained. Next time, he'll be carrying a gun."

He didn't know it at the time, but his Karloff movie was already beginning to take shape.

CHAPTER 8

October 1966 (1)

It happened to be raining in Los Angeles and well before Roger's arrival when Frances' typing was interrupted by an unusually early telephone call. "Good morning, Corman Company."

"Top o' the morning, Precious."

The voice, and its sly warmth, had become familiar to her over the past weeks, as Jack Nicholson kept them abreast of the rewrite's development. He always took a little extra time to flirt. Unbeknownst to her, the pillow talk he imparted on this particular morning arose less from casual amorousness than from an almost primal urgency to rest his head on one. In order to meet the agreed-upon deadline, which happened to be this very day, he had been writing for the last two days without sleep. He was buzzing.

"Listen, Precious, tell your boss that I'm fully aware of what day it is and the nature of the promise attached to it. To be perfectly honest, I am not done yet but the day has just begun. It is remotely—I say, remotely—possible I may edge over into a little overtime, I almost said Ovaltine, but if that happens, it will be over my dead or sleeping body, whichever comes first. Conversely, my fair lady, the ending is well in sight. I'm gonna try my proverbial damnedest to finish up today, though I am concerned about the quality of polish I might be able to bring to this thing if I had a few hours' sleep behind me. Maybe I'll take, you know, just a little crash to refresh my batteries. I'd really like to come back at this and hit it—and hit it hard. At the same time, I'd really like to have this in Roger's hands by the end of the day. I'm only calling because I know you get into the office early, and all this sad sack apology is going to sound a hell of a lot nicer coming from you than it'll sound coming from me, you know? Oh, and Frankie, please tell him from me that I think it's good, really good stuff—*serious* stuff—and I will do everything within my power to have it ready for him by the end of business today. This page I'm stuck on, I've used enough white-out to paint a snow scene, and I could swear there was a mistake I made back on page 67 that I overlooked, but hell if I can find it. I'll try to give it one last once-over before I hand it in. No, that's no good, better to turn in, hit the hay for an hour or two, and then come back to it with a clear head, or at least a clearer…"

"Stop, stop, stop!" Frances protested through her giggling. "I can't absorb all that you're saying! What is it about this script that turns people into word monsters?"

"I guess that colors me done, then. With this call, anyway."

"I'll give Roger the message, Jack. Thank you for calling."

"Ta very much."

At 9:30 a.m., Roger strode into the office, whistling a song, folding his umbrella and shaking the rain off of his bucket hat. "Good morning, Frances!"

He headed for his office, with Frances close behind. She deposited some envelopes on his desk and held one apart, waving it.

"The mailman delivered this invoice from your alienist: 'Final Billing.' You're not seeing her anymore?"

"We came to a point," Roger explained, while tackling his breakfast tray. "She told me that I wasn't going to change because I don't really want to change. Toast?"

She accepted a triangular slice of buttered wheat toast and chewed it silently for a few seconds.

"Every morning," she then observed, "without fail or variation, you arrive at 9:30 and have the same breakfast. Scrambled eggs, wheat toast. Then for lunch, your Metrecal. You dress more or less the same every day.

The furniture in here has never been moved around. You've been making movies for American International now for... how long?"

"Since *The Fast and the Furious,* 1955. Their first picture. My third."

"Even the things about you that change do so at a predictable rate. It seems you have a new dolly-bird on your arm every couple of weeks..."

"That's change, isn't it?"

"...and you've increased your picture-to-picture profits at almost exactly 10% gross with each new production."

Roger enjoyed this observation best of all. The phone rang.

"Go ahead, take it here," Roger allowed.

Frances answered the call. "Corman Company. Oh, hello, Jack...I thought you were grabbing some winks...Yes, he's in now...Okay then, I'll tell him. Cut it out. I mean it—I'm working. Of course. Ta!" She hung up.

She brought Roger up to speed: "Jack. He phoned earlier, wanted you to know he'd not forgotten his deadline. He said he was having some trouble wrapping things up, but promised to deliver a.s.a.p. Now it seems he's had a breakthrough and should have something for you as early as 3:00 this afternoon. Poor thing. Sounds like he hasn't had head to pillow in days."

It was a slow day at the office, so Roger grabbed his bucket hat around 3:00 and headed out into the lessening rain. On his way to Jack's place, he listened to a new 8-track acquisition, Julie London's *Julie Is Her Name.* He noticed that music sounded better in his Mercedes with the top up. "Cry Me A River" went so well with the weather.

When he pulled up outside the Stanton house, he found Jack standing on the porch—looking like one of the shipwrecked from a Jules Verne novel. He stood there, shirtless, in wrinkled shorts and sandals, with unwashed and prematurely thinning hair in need of barbering, and at least a week's growth of beard. He clutched a fat manila envelope to his chest. And, in the words of the poet, his eyes were wild.

"You finished?" Roger asked hopefully, approaching the porch.

"I finished," Jack triumphed, patting the envelope like a proud, if somewhat dazed, papa.

"I look forward to reading it." Roger reached out to take receipt of it, but Jack continued to clutch it to his chest. "Is something wrong, Jack?"

"I'm sorry, Roger. I know you're a busy man and in a hurry, but there's something important I feel I have to express before I hand this over and send you on your merry way."

"Tell me."

Jack furrowed his scrub board brow, bit his lower lip and turned, strolling around the bend of the porch and heading towards its rear balcony. Roger had little choice but to follow.

The rain had by now stopped. There were vestiges of precipitation—wet foliage, dripping leaves, dripping eaves—but the sky had largely cleared. Jack went to the porch rail overlooking the valley, placed the bundled script on an outdoor table, and cast his scratchy, sandy-eyed gaze over the valley below.

Roger cautiously took a seat on the swing, moving a folded section of newspaper aside to make room for himself. There was a serious headline that caught his eye—something about France performing a nuclear test on Moruroa atoll—but, for the moment, Jack required his fullest attention.

"Roger," Jack began, "I know this project is primarily an exploitation picture to you. I don't say this critically, merely as a statement of fact. No offense intended."

"None taken."

"Now that's it, right there," he said, seizing upon Roger's assurance with a divining finger. "'None taken.' 'None taken' is what I need to talk with you about."

"Go on."

"Roger, I agreed to do this job for purely mercenary reasons, no bones about it... but this has become more than just a movie to me. My blood... my brain... my bowels are invested in this now."

"Oh, Jack."

"I don't mean to go all D.H. Lawrence on ya, but Roger, hear me out. This movie could turn out real bad, unless..."

"Unless what?"

Jack replied with child-like simplicity: "Unless you drop acid."

"What!?"

"Call it research."

"Jack, I've done my homework," Roger protested. "I've read all the leading books on the subject."

"But homework ain't experience, man!" Jack nearly screamed. "I'm sorry," he immediately apologized, reeling himself back in. "How the fuck do I explain this?"

Jack turned once again to the view as if in search of an answer among all the foliage and treetops and coyote howls below, then turned slowly around to face Roger once again.

"You see all this? *This* and *this* and *this* and *this*?" He illustrated each of those points as he spoke by gesturing to the view, gripping the porch rail, patting the script on the table and slapping the painted exterior of Harry Dean's house. "Of course you don't!

"It's not really there," Jack continued, "but believe me, you feel it weighing down on you, every single goddamn day. It's called 'reality.' And reality piles up . . . like novocaine. It dulls the senses."

Initially concerned, Roger was now absolutely charmed by this performance, realizing that Jack had just quoted two of the lines he had spoken in *The Little Shop of Horrors*—the first time he had actually directed Jack in a picture. He leaned back to enjoy the show.

Jack paced back and forth, railing like some kind of Skid Row messiah: "You're born, you crap your diapers, you get into long pants, you toss the old ball around and, as day turns to day turns to year after year, you start to take all the miracles in this world for granted. You meet a lady, you like the look of her, you get married. You stay married. The years pass, and suddenly it's like you can't see her because you can't see where she ends and you begin. Familiarity breeds . . . it ain't contempt, it's more like *blindness*. But acid . . . Roger, acid kinda brings you back into *your own presence*. Into the presence of all things." He leaned close to Roger, peering into his eyes. "You don't just smell the roses . . . you . . . *understand* the roses. Put it that way."

"What about addiction? Isn't that an issue?"

Jack tossed the newspaper section aside and sat next to Roger, assuming a choirboy's demeanor. "Acid is *not* addictive, Roger. Hand to heart."

"How about mental damage?"

Suddenly, Jack was back on his feet, hooting and hollering. "Ya damn fool! It's crazier to make a movie about acid than it is to actually take the stuff!"

Jack paused for a moment, trying very hard to reground himself. "Hey, I don't deny there's a modicum of risk involved. Most of these you can easily minimize. If you don't want to go walking through a plate glass window, stay away from plate glass windows. If you don't want to jump off a roof because you think you can fly, stay off the roof. Just common sense. And know this: no matter how many safeguards you provide yourself, you *still* might not necessarily like what you see. But I can promise you this, my friend. You'll come away a bit wiser. You'll see and know yourself and the world around you in ways you never thought possible. I'm talking heavy, heavy changes, man."

Roger perked up, leaning forward.

"Did you say... *changes*?"

With this persuasive and resonant word in mind, Roger proceeded to read Jack's refreshingly concise but insistently otherly script. Each turned page seemed to take him to the edge of a precipice from which he had no choice but to leap. Were this challenge presented to him as solely a life choice, he might be able to ignore it, but this gauntlet was being thrown down at his feet in the arenas of art and business.

He had broken off with Dr. Xavier because she found him stubbornly resistant to necessary changes in his character, in his nature; he could plainly see the evidence of this resistance in the merry-go-round nature of his dating life, and in the fact that he was continuing to make films within the comfort zone of his uncomfortable relationship with American International, even though he was working out of an office on the lot of a major Hollywood studio impatiently awaiting the pitch that would certify him as a major player. In both cases, he was not exactly afraid—but wary of the consequences that might result were he to step off their revolving wheels onto solid ground. Because he had been refusing to make such decisions on his own, even with professional help, the world around him was now conspiring to force his hand.

Was it really necessary that he take LSD in order to make a film about it? Internally, he argued the point: it would be possible to make a film about heroin addiction without actually using heroin because the results of its use and addiction are so plainly observable from the outside. LSD, however, was something different. It didn't necessarily brand someone who had used it as an obvious user. Its effects appeared to be tailor-made to the individual. As a filmmaker, he felt reasonably sure that he had what he needed to make his movie. But what he had on paper, in a filmable number of pages, was Jack's trip. The more he thought about it, it did need to be his own.

Naturally, he felt some trepidation. The documentation he had consulted acknowledged the possibility of "bad trips" and it seemed that, when- ever he was assured there was no danger of becoming addicted, the assurance came from someone who had done acid two or three hundred times.

The more he ruminated on the matter, the more he found himself remembering the time when he and his crew went out to Charleston and those other towns in Missouri to make *The Intruder* back in 1962. That took nerve, to live and work for those weeks in a hotbed of racism, back-wardness, and pending violence, to pretend to be making a film in support of what they were actually against, relying on the color of his own skin to misrepresent his true intentions. Each day down there brought with it the possibility of discovery, imprisonment, even trial in one of their kangaroo courts. He remembered the phrase "necktie party" being passed around in filthy chuckles. Because of the risks taken by he and his companions, *The Intruder* became a statement about the fear that underlies all hate, which he had never before experienced so personally.

Thoughts of this period easily segued into his more recent experience of earning and placating the trust of the Hell's Angels during the production of *The Wild Angels*. It had been his goal to make a film about them that was entirely objective and without judgment. Though he felt he had succeeded at this, the Angels themselves seemed to disagree. Perhaps their stance on the matter had nothing to do with him at all, but rather with something Marlon Brando had once said in *The Wild One*: "What are you rebelling against?" "Whaddya got?"

Even the Poe films he had made from Richard Matheson's finely expansive scripts had benefited indirectly from Roger's discovery of Poe's original stories in childhood. Nothing in those scripts, good as they were, could have told him how to be the traffic cop on those sets, deciding which furniture, which tapestries, which colors were appropriate and which would have been completely wrong. From a distance of decades, Poe's language had somehow lodged in his creative DNA, though he rarely refreshed his memory of the stories themselves.

The more he pondered the matter, weak and weary, he was confronted with the inevitability that the only way he would be truly capable of interpreting Jack's script—*Jack's trip*—was to take his own.

Roger began to plan for his trip the way he would plan for any trip from place to place. First, he had to settle on a destination. Dr. Timothy Leary's book *The Psychedelic Experience* had impressed upon him the necessity of framing one's experience in a setting of beauty and tranquility. He cast his thoughts wide, thinking back to the most beautiful places he had ever been. He had been all over the world—San Francisco was a gorgeous city but too urban; the Grand Canyon was a tempting prospect until he realized that, in an altered state, it might appear indistinguishable from the drop off a 10-story building and prove frighteningly irresistible; Dubrovnik was sunny, picturesque and spectacular but it was also behind the Iron Curtain, an association his research implied it might not be wise to psychedelicize. He briefly considered a return to his childhood home in Detroit, Michigan, but the whole idea quickly felt inverted; the point of all this was not returning to the womb, but rather bursting out of one's present chrysalis. Furthermore, any expenses incurred would be coming directly out of budget so he came to the conclusion that anything involving air travel would be impractical for him and detrimental to the movie.

As Roger began thinking closer to home, closer to now, he pictured the different beaches along Pacific Coast Highway—locations he had used in the opening sequences of the Poe films, for example—but, attractive and convenient as many of them were, in his mind they represented the shackles of work rather than freedom, and they were also likely to be densely populated round the clock given their proximity to town.

Big Sur began to assert itself in his thoughts as inevitable. It truly was the most majestic natural spot on Earth that he knew, and sufficiently remote from Los Angeles and San Francisco to discourage most visitors. It was likely to be still more deserted if he happened to choose a weekday for his inner space adventure.

Once he had settled on the destination, Roger began to think of travelling companions. Leary asserted the absolute importance of tripping with a trusted guide. Oddly enough, Julie was the first person who came to mind—because, during their first dinner together, for no better reason than to make conversation, she had surprised him with the question, "Who's your best friend?" The question surprised him because he honestly couldn't recall anyone putting it to him before. He thought for a moment and told her "Chuck Griffith"—and proceeded to tell her things about him that made her laugh, sometimes because the story was funny or outrageous but sometimes because Roger's rollicking account of his friendship with Chuck added a further, pleasing dimension to her own evolving understanding of the man she was with. He could see this in her face. With this in mind, Roger resolved that Chuck—someone already "experienced"—would function as his "guide" and that Frances should also be present to observe from a sober, detached perspective and take thorough, time-coded notes on whatever transpired.

His instincts told him this was not something to mention to Julie. She had been terrified by the idea of him working with Hell's Angels and somehow, through the brotherhood of beer, he had managed to keep out of bodily contact with them. The risk in this instance would be something he would ingest, take into his own body, and for some reason he felt he couldn't embark on such an adventure if it was met by her disapproval. So, Julie was to be kept out of the loop. Business was business.

Finally, Roger scrutinized his desk calendar for the perfect date for the trip and decided on October 11, 1966. It would be a Tuesday and Tuesdays at the office were always slow. Frances was amused to note that, for Roger, organizing the day was remarkably like scheduling a new picture.

Once the details of time and destination were settled and shared on a need-to-know basis, they began to circulate in the form of incredulous confidences and excited whispers. As the date approached, Frances found herself fielding phone calls from some of Roger's acquaintances, people within his production circle who ran the gamut from aging beatniks, nascent hippies, and UCLA film school graduates, to many of whom he'd given important career breaks—all excited by the news and asking if they might tag along. Frances informed Roger with some embarrassment. However, envisioning himself at the head of a small, supportive caravan was not unpleasant, so Roger made it clear to Frances that, while he liked in general the idea of engendering an atmosphere of bonhomie at Big Sur, this was a matter of research rather than recreation. Frances narrowed their train to half a dozen or so friends who could follow them up, share meals and such, but keep a respectful distance at the time of "take-off," as Chuck called it. Generally speaking, the identities of these fellow travelers have remained privileged information, with the exception of Sharon Compton—friend of the company, production coordinator on *The Wild Angels* and wardrobe wrangler on some cheaper productions. Sharon was pregnant at the time and would not be partaking, but she was fascinated and curious, and—perhaps most importantly—one of those people everyone liked and felt good around. Her delicate condition could only enhance the natural aura of her nurturing spirit.

Then, in the midst of these and other preparations, Frances received a call that threatened to change the tenor of the entire undertaking.

It was the afternoon of October 6th—the Thursday before the Tuesday when Roger's trip was scheduled—when Jack Nicholson rang up. Frances recognized the Irishman's voice but he was not his usual flirtatious self; she could hear immediately in the unusual flatness of his tone that something was seriously amiss. No "Top o' the Morning," no "Precious." Had his car finally died? Did his electricity get turned off?

"Jack, what's wrong?"

"Maybe everything. I'm just lookin' at the morning paper. My eye was caught by these pictures of Ronald Reagan and Pat Brown. You never saw two happier, haler-looking mother-lovers, pattin' each other's backs. They just made acid illegal in California state."

"You're joking!"

"Do I sound like a joker? Isn't this just my luck? Goddamn it, I wrote that script in good faith. Now, I admit, I did it for the money, but I also thought, if I told the truth as I saw it, it just might help some people. Now people are gonna get scared off. The government's gonna make them afraid. All they're gonna see is a movie about contraband."

"Oh, Jack, this is terrible."

"I was hoping for some inside scoop," he explained, edgily. "Is this gonna bollox everything up? Am I screwed? I mean, I got half my money up front on delivery, but I don't get the other half till this picture starts shootin'... Am I ever gonna see it?"

"Let me share this with Roger, Jack," she pleaded. "I promise to get right back to you."

"I'll be here," he said with crushed finality.

Frances hung up the telephone, feeling as though the bottom had fallen out of her stomach, along with all their carefully made plans.

She rapped lightly on Roger's open door. He was seated behind his desk, of course, paging through the current issue of *Scientific American*.

"What's the matter?" he asked, reading something unsteady in her expression. "Not Hell's Angels again?"

She approached his desk. "Roger, Jack just called. The state of California has just banned the use of LSD."

Roger slapped the magazine shut. "Really?"

"I'm afraid so."

For a moment, Roger looked as though someone offstage had flicked a switch that turned off all the gravity in the world. He planted his feet firmly on the floor and the flats of his hands firmly on his desk as he looked around for something grounded to hang onto. "I suppose this will endear Pat Brown to a few more Reaganites," he managed, pensively.

He picked up a No. 2 pencil and began drumming on the desktop. "But I am not surprised..." The snare of the calendar, the tom-tom of the telephone.

He thought to himself: *This is terrible. But wait a minute. Let's take stock. What has really happened? A politician has spoken (and possibly lost my support). A law has been changed. LSD has been made illegal. But... it has not been obliterated. It has merely changed vendors, driven underground. But things can happen underground. Just like things can happen in a Roger Corman picture.*

He tapped the cymbal of his caliper with righteous authority. "... and, all things considered," he summarized, "I am *not* displeased."

Frances regarded him with incredulity. "You're not? But isn't this a disaster?"

"Think about it, Frances," Roger explained. "If you were a teenager, which would you prefer to see a movie about? A drug you could obtain from your family doctor... or the drug that's in the headlines, the one the United States government doesn't want you to have?"

Like that, her emotional response began to recalibrate. "Okay," she said, aligning herself to this new viewpoint. "That's all well and good for the movie... but what about our plans for next week?"

"So long as we're not imprudent about our intentions, I see no reason why our plans should change."

"So, we're still moving ahead? Still going?"

"Worst case scenario?" Roger threw out his arms like Christ crucified and brought his wrists clashing together in imaginary manacles. Then he unleashed his most irresistible grin. "Hollywood Director Busted at Big Sur! Film at Eleven!"

CHAPTER 9

OCTOBER 1966 (2)

"OH, JESUS. JESUS H. CHRIST."

"Baby, are you crying?"

"I've got to tell him."

"You mean right now?"

"My script? Which one?"

"The one you wrote for Roger Corman . . . The Trip . . . You've brought the French New Wave to the Pacific! You've put D.W. Griffith on mescalin!"

"I did? Well, won't the folks back home be proud! . . . Film is a dying art form."

"I say we kill it or cure it."

It was early afternoon. When Frances buzzed him, Roger was seated at his desk, trying to make some headway through the local library's copy of Alan W. Watts' *The Joyous Cosmology*.

"Yes, Frances?"

"Roger, Peter Fonda's here to . . . Oops, coming through!"

Peter burst into his office, all smiles, his lanky form approaching him with hand outstretched. Roger was taken aback, in a bracing sort of way. In the split-second before Peter spoke, Roger flashed back to the day of their first meeting, when Peter came in to talk about doing *The Wild Angels*—at the time, a script only partly written. He had arrived more or less in character, wearing denim, an Iron Cross, and a leather jacket studded with assorted anti-establishment buttons and patches. There was also a badge of some sort.

"What's the badge for?" Roger had asked, hoping to break the ice.

Without missing a beat, Peter had said, "That gives me permission to piss on your tires."

Then as now, the air around Peter Fonda was perpetually charged with drama, hazard, a heightened sense of quest, all of which he sought to discharge with a down-to-earth sense of humor aimed back at the whole crazy circus of life.

"Peter," Roger opened, "what a nice surprise! I take it you've read the script?"

"I did," he answered. "Did you?"

"Of course," Roger smiled; a bit confused. "I commissioned it, I read it, I approved it and had it sent to you. You're Paul Groves."

"You read it, but . . . did you understand it? Or did it understand you?"

"I don't understand what you're asking."

Peter leaned forward, earnestly. "Did you understand everything the script was putting forward, or did you just empathize with the character and his struggle?"

"In all honesty, perhaps the latter," Roger admitted. "The details in the script, I suspect, are rooted in Jack's personal experience, which is not exactly mine."

Peter responded approvingly. "Groovy. That's what I wanted to hear. You're being on the level with me, and I've never known you to be anything else. But I was concerned that this material might be somewhat out of your depth. It's one thing to follow the directions laid down in a script, going A to Z, but this script is a special case, a very special case. With this, you need to know how to get from A to 2, if you get my meaning. And if you can't, because you are out of your element, then you're fucked. You, me, the movie. We're all fucked. This is not your ordinary script. Every busboy in town has one of those at home, sitting cold in a dark drawer. But this isn't your usual Boy Meets Girl or Spaceman Lands on Earth bullshit. This is opportunity. This is responsibility. We're talking sacred duty."

Roger, keeping his eyes on the solemn actor, reached for his intercom. "Frances, hold my calls."

Peter fell silent for almost a full minute, so when he continued speaking Roger's ears were acutely attuned to the sound of his voice.

"Roger, I got really emotional reading Jack's script. Usually, I read a script, I look at a role, and my response is 'How can I play this?' But when I read this, it was actually... pertinent. It was crucial. I was like, 'How can I *not* play this?' This could change everything. You know that phrase from Aldous Huxley, 'the doors of perception'? Where that group The Doors got their name? This could tear that door off its hinges. It could change people. Because young people will go in to see this, and when it's all over, there is so much they'll want to do with their lives. They will suddenly be so alert to its potential. But there's one thing they won't have any interest in doing, and that's picking up a rifle to kill people in 'Nam. They're gonna know that what's most essential is life. They're going to assess their lives and ask themselves if this is the way they want to live, or if there's another, better way. And awareness. They're gonna want to breathe the air and feel the grass beneath their feet. And love, making contact with someone who, who is the essence of life to them." Suddenly, unexpectedly, he laughed. "But why am I telling you all this? I mean, this came from you; you must know all this. I just have to know, man... what is this script to you?"

Roger took a moment to boil his convoluted thoughts down to their barest essentials. "It's a three-week shoot, starting after the holidays, that it has to be in theaters by..." He rifled through the pages of his desktop calendar. "...August 23, 1967."

"Whoa, man," Peter said, inserting an upraised hand into the space between their faces, as if warding off something unexpected and unwelcome. "With apologies to the poet, there's something happening here, and what it is ain't exactly clear."

"I'm not sure I understand you, Peter," Roger responded. "What sort of assurance do you need from me?"

"You know, when Jack told me you would be directing, I have to be honest—I had my doubts. When we did *The Wild Angels* together, you hadn't even smoked pot. You haven't done acid either, I'm guessing."

"That's right; I haven't."

"You're a strange case, my friend. You're kind of a square, you color inside all the lines, but look at all these posters on your walls from the films you've made! Not one of them represents an Establishment mind."

"I'll take that as a compliment."

"I'm not trying to be complimentary, man," Peter clarified. "I'm trying to bring you to your own attention. Because I don't know that you were ever conscious of that fact about yourself. This script requires you be in direct contact with yourself. If you can manage that, there will be times, there will be pages, when you'll be required to color outside the lines Jack has provided, because that will be the key to *you* making it personal, to *you* making it real. If you can't do that, you'll not only blow the chance of a lifetime, your audience might never trust you again. So dig: This movie is a trip I'd love to take. I'm ready to go a mile out on a limb for you, Roger, but I'll need you as my guide. Will you be out there on that limb with me?"

Roger didn't know what to say to this. He made a candidly helpless gesture in response.

Peter became more direct. "Why are you making this film?"

"Honestly," Roger confessed, "I'm making this film to solve a problem."

"What problem is that?"

"The same problem that's proposed by any picture. How to turn $300,000 into several millions. Parden me: $450,000. The success of *The Wild Angels* has bumped us up to more comfortable quarters."

"You're honest," Peter appraised. "I can dig that. Don't get me wrong, I grew up in this freaky business and know what it's about; I'm not against success. But this script draws a line in the sand and I have to be sure which side of that line you're on. I need to know you're committed to telling the truth about acid. I need you to know that truth."

"You think I should actually take L... S... D before I film this script?"

"I do."

"Well, it's funny you should say that, Peter... because I plan to."

"On the level?"

"Absolutely," Roger said, paging forward a couple of days in his desktop calendar and holding it up for his guest's edification.

"What's that?" Peter chuckled. "An itinerary?"

"That's a perfectly good word for it."

"No shit?"

"Roger always says what he means," Frances said from the open doorway.

And like that, the uncomfortable, confrontational energy accumulating in the room was dispelled.

"Groovy," Peter summarized. "Well! Seeing that you have an itinerary, I'm proud to be aboard. Happy sailing!"

Peter shook Roger's hand in parting and ambled toward the open door, where he paused and looked back. "By the way, our governor—in his wisdom—just made finding the stuff a bit harder for you. You have a connection? Because I could . . . "

"A connection?"

"Peter means, do you have a source for obtaining the drug?" Frances clarified.

"I do, thanks," Roger grinned. "My therapist had to withdraw her assistance for legal reasons, but we have a back-up plan."

"I can't believe you need me to score acid for you," Chuck Griffith chided. "Why didn't you just ask Fonda?"

"My friend Peter," Roger reasoned, "is a zealous advocate of mind-altering chemicals. So zealous, in fact, that I fear his judgment may be fogged in relation to . . . "

Chuck cut in: "You think he'll jack your dosage."

"Correct."

"Whereas he trusts you, Chuck!" Frances interjected.

"He trusts me with this, but he won't use my screenplay?"

"It was a wonderful screenplay," Roger schmoozed. "Extremely creative. Ask Frances if I didn't say so!"

"If he loved mine so much, why did he go to Nicholson for a rewrite?"

"Well," Frances feebly began.

The Venice Boardwalk was a dreary stretch of dirty sand, traversed by surfers, carnival goers, narcissistic muscle-flexers, Hollywood hopefuls crammed into bikinis, stubble-faced jugglers, and haunted-looking drifters on the prowl for dropped wallets. A loud radio somewhere pounded the Felliniesque environs with Sonny and Cher's "The Beat Goes On." Roger was walking almost parallel with Chuck, his guide into this strange netherworld, while Frances straggled a few steps behind, rooting around in her purse. She found her sunglasses, and now all three of them were similarly disguised for this excursion into unfamiliar terrain.

At some point, as they made their uncertain way through the living Pop Art collage that was Venice Beach, Chuck suddenly responded to the setting like a hunting dog and began walking with a greater sense of direction and specificity. Roger had trained himself to look several steps ahead in all things, so it was fairly easy for him to determine that their ultimate goal was a simple shack on the beach, filled with and surrounded by myriad potted exotic flora for sale. Hawking these wares from a cheap beach chair was an old Beatnik, 65 if he was a day, resplendently goateed and decked out in Bermuda shorts, a flowered Hawaiian shirt, red-lensed shades, and a gray Fedora. He looked almost too conspicuous to be functionally inconspicuous.

"Is that the dealer?" Roger asked, as though addressing a crowd over the roar of the surf.

"Jesus, Roger!" Chuck exclaimed. "Pipe down, willya?"

"I mean our 'connection'?"

"Not a 'dealer,' not a 'connection.' Manny's a mensch, Roger. He only sells soft stuff. Now go shut up and hide."

Roger and Frances held back, but Chuck came back and took Frances by the arm. "Not you," he told her, "—him. You may actually be helpful. Manny has an eye for the ladies."

"Very well," she agreed.

"Why can't I take part?" Roger objected petulantly.

Chuck walked back to him. "Because you'll scare him away. Roger, you look so much like a narc, you make *me* nervous!"

"You're over-reacting. I haven't had a haircut in three weeks," he objected.

"Excuse me. An *undercover* narc."

It was at this point when Manny first caught sight of them. "Is that you, Chuckles?" he called out. "My man!"

"Manny!" Chuck called back, rushing over to greet him. Frances hovered midway between the shack and Roger, who held back, observing with mild jealousy as the two hipsters gripped hands fraternally, then crunched together in an embrace.

"What goes on, Manny?" asked Chuck.

"Here I stand, in my prime, teenage surfer girls all around me."

"Testify, brother."

"Long tangerine-colored legs turned golden brown by the blessed California sun," he added with the mournful measures of the advanced middle-aged.

Manny looked around, furtively, and noticed Roger hovering, furtively. Then he added, more covertly: "Hey, you shopping today, Chuckles? I got leaves, I got buds. Lots plants cheap, you dig?"

Chuck looked over his shoulder to his two friends and waved Frances over. "Hello," she said meekly, clutching her purse.

"Manny," Chuck said, "this is my friend... Doris."

Manny promptly stepped out of his shack and bowed deeply, kissing Frances on the hand. "A pleasure to meet you, fair lady!" he said. "Such a balm to these world-weary eyes."

"Why, aren't you charming!" she smiled.

"And what a voice!"

"How sweet."

Chuck adjusted his volume a tad as he shifted into sly business mode. "Hey, Manny, we're thinkin' of driving up the PCH this weekend, hittin' some beaches. Thought we'd—you know—get a little... *sunshine?* Got any party favors?"

"How many are we talking? 75? 150? 300?"

"300 would cover it."

"Can you help us?" Frances cut in.

Manny looked at Chuck. "For him?" He blew a loud raspberry, then laughed to prove it was all in fun. "But for you, young lady... the Moon! The Moon, I say!"

"Yeah?" Chuck said, excited. "How much?"

"I can shave a hair or two off the going rate. I'll give you the cubic rate. For you, five per cube."

"Oh, man," Chuck groused. "Five?"

Manny beckoned Chuck to kneel down within whispering range. He enfolded him with the hirsute arm poking out from the exploding flora of his Hawaiian shirt. He spoke warmly and intimately. "These are primo cubes, amigo. Owsleys!"

Chuck was a writer who lived from paycheck to paycheck. He didn't know from negotiation. He caved in and began reaching for his wallet, which was more than Roger could bear. As Chuck started reaching for his wallet, he stepped forward into the midst of the interaction and brought it to the proverbial screeching halt.

"That'll do, Chuck."

At the sight of him, Manny shriveled.

"Who the fuck is *this?*" he asked of the cosmos, or Chuck, whichever heard him first. "Mister, you got *nuthin'* on me! This guy mistook me for someone else! Get away from me, young fella, I don't know you."

Frances now intervened. "Mr. Manny, let me introduce you. This is Roger Corman, and I'm his personal assistant, Frances Doel."

Manny turned to glower accusingly at Chuck. "I thought you were Doris! What the hell *is* this?"

Roger held up his hands in a friendly, calming gesture. "Allow me to explain, Mr. Manny. This is our situation. My name *is* Roger Corman. I am not an officer of the law, nor is the substance we are hoping to procure to be used for scurrilous, purely recreational purposes. The fact is, I require your illicit product because I am planning a major Hollywood picture on the subject of its use."

Manny looked from one set of sunglasses to another, befuddled by all that he was hearing.

"It is not my intention to cheat you," Roger continued, "but every dime we spend on supplies detracts a dime from the larger purpose of the picture itself. Therefore, the nature of this transaction is restricted."

"Hey," Manny growled, "I don't even know you!"

"True," Roger confirmed. "But imagine the almost limitless source you will have tapped into, once you have availed us of what we require for the sum of, I'm thinking, one dollar and fifty cents per unit."

Manny's bearded jaw dropped.

"A buck fifty? For Owsleys? Are you off your grandma's rocker?"

"A dollar fifty now," Roger concurred, presenting the larger picture. "But imagine how much business will come your way after this entrée into the movie-making community with its many well-to-do performers."

"That's enough," Manny grumbled. To Roger: "You—fuck off." To Frances: "You—pardon my French." To Chuck: "He's crazy, Chuckles."

Roger thought fast. "Alright, Chuck—I didn't think this was going to work. Why don't we just go up to La Brea, as I originally suggested, and see that other guy who said he could obtain the best at cost—for a screen credit. What did he say the cost was?"

"I was told a dollar seventy-five per unit," Frances said.

Manny suddenly acquired the look of a man waking from a disorienting dream. "Screen credit? *My name on the screen?*"

"It might be possible," Roger allowed. "For one *seventy* per unit."

"And what would this screen credit say?"

"Mr. Manny," answered Roger, "that credit will read... 'Associate Producer'."

CHAPTER 10

October 1966 (3)

After putting in half of a workday (Roger insisted), his little caravanserai set off for Big Sur on the afternoon of Monday, October 10th, along the northward stretch of Highway 101. Roger took the lead behind the wheel of his Mercedes. He was cheerfully admiring the coastal scenery as an overhead sign passed by: BIG SUR, 150 MILES.

Frances occupied the passenger seat, reading aloud from the notes she had taken on various library books, while Chuck Griffith—still pleasantly buzzed from the roach he'd had with breakfast—was curled up in the back seat with a well-loved paperback of *Dr. Sax* by Jack Kerouac. He had stowed his tent in the boot of Roger's car, brought along on the reasonable assumption that there would be no room for him at the Inn. He had been turned away by a few hotels, even motels, in his day—simply for the way he looked. *Their loss*, he philosophized. *It's better to crash on the beach.*

There was a momentary lull in Frances' recital. "Yes, go on," Roger encouraged.

"Hang on, I'm trying to make sense here of my sleepy handwriting. Okay... It's called *The Tibetan Book of the Dead*. The Beatles specifically reference it in two of their songs, 'Tomorrow Never Knows' and 'I'm Only Sleeping.' It's called *The Book of the Dead* because its instructions are intended for the recently deceased."

"Like *The Lawrence Welk Show*," Chuck interjected.

"I don't understand," Roger said. "Why the emphasis on death in the context of an LSD trip? That would seem to be the opposite of my objective."

Frances began rifling through her pages of scrawls. "I have an explanation, hold on a sec... Yes, here it is. Oh, I see. It's not to be confused with Death in a mortal sense but rather in a transitive one. As with the Tarot card. In other words, during the course of one's trip, one experiences *a death of the Ego*, a necessary relinquishment of the Self. You may think you're dying, but you won't actually die—you'll simply, er, pass through to a state of heightened awareness."

"Chuck, you've taken this journey before," Roger observed. "What's your experience of this?"

"There is that," he concurred. "Also bugs and funny-colored Jell-O."

"We should probably give some thought to tomorrow's timetable," Frances suggested, changing the subject to more practical matters.

Roger had already planned the day. "The trip is supposed to last approximately eight hours, so I would like to get started no later than 8:00 in the morning, which will allow us to finish by 4:00 in the afternoon, at the latest. Then we can head right back to LA."

"What, no lunch break?" Chuck sniped.

By the time Caravan Corman reached their destination at the Big Sur Inn on Highway One, Roger was worn out from the five-hour drive and all the last-minute instruction that came with it. After spending some obligatory time with his friends, together appreciating the location's boundless scenic beauty, he began to feel a strange, inexplicable emptiness and the need for a little preparatory solitude. He apologized to the others if it made him seem a poor host, but he opted not to join them for dinner that night at the Inn's restaurant, even though it was built into the side of a ridge and looked out over the sweeping waves of the great Pacific.

Alone in his room, on the eve of his great adventure, Roger wondered if this was how the NASA astronauts felt on the eve of an important mission—a state of mind so singular, perhaps so sacred, it couldn't really be shared with other people—or was he feeling this way because he hadn't shared this moment with the right person? There was a point in their preparations for the trip that Frances had asked him if there was someone special he'd like to invite along. No sooner was the question asked than a face, a look, a voice, a laugh did materialize in his mind—but an occasion such as this wasn't really the right opportunity, the right reason, to renew contact.

To help deflect his thoughts, he phoned the front desk and asked if they might arrange for the use of a portable television set. About ten minutes later, a teenage boy promptly delivered a black-and-white model, who was given the tip of Roger's personal thanks.

As serendipity would have it, no sooner had he plugged in the set and dialed through the few available channels—floor wax commercial, courtroom drama rerun, Vietnam death toll—than Roger happened to spot his old friend Vincent Price wearing a lab coat in what appeared to be a private examination room. The coincidence felt like glad tidings.

There was a brisk knock at the door.

Roger opened the door and found Frances standing there with a few aromatic boxes. "I know you said you weren't hungry," she smiled, "but the food was so good, we thought a doggie bag might be welcome."

"That's most thoughtful, Frances," Roger grinned. "Thank you."

"It's a bit of the Inn's famous prime rib with *au jus*, baked potato with salted skins and butter, sweet caramelized carrots, and your customary gin martini—regrettably served in a carry-out cup."

"You think of everything."

Frances looked beyond Roger to the movie playing on the television set. "Vincent!" she exclaimed. The debonair actor rolled up the sleeve of his lab coat and injected himself with a hypodermic syringe. "One of yours?"

Roger shook his head negatively. "The competition."

"Well, you're welcome to join us down on the beach. A couple of the others brought guitars so we'll be having a little hootenanny before turning in. I know you said 8:00 a.m. sharp, so I'll keep an eye on the time and call a stop to the merriment no later than 11:00."

"Excellent."

"Where shall we meet in the morning?"

Roger thought for a moment. "Do you know the waterfall?"

"Lovely choice! Alright, then. Good night, Roger."

"Sleep well, Frances!" he said as she closed the door behind her. "Tell the others to have fun. I'll see them in the morning."

Roger took the plastic cap off the paper cup that held his martini and took a sip—not bad, considering its homely presentation. He wasn't happy about the ice cubes but a martini served straight-up wouldn't last very long otherwise inside a paper cup. Then he peeked inside the carryout boxes at his dinner, which looked reasonably appetizing—but he wasn't feeling particularly hungry. What was eating him?

His arms hung limp at his sides, his hands feeling empty and heavy when—suddenly—his right hand slapped the pocket where he kept his wallet. Its abrupt movement wasn't exactly involuntarily so much as guided by a will stronger than his conscious mind. He removed his wallet, unfolded it, and took out a carefully folded piece of paper. On the paper, in his own handwriting, was a name and telephone number. As soon as he saw the inscription, all the loose tetherings, all the unanswered signals in his being seemed to pull together, tautly, toward a common purpose.

He went to the telephone on the bedside table and read the instructions about how to dial an outside line. He sat on his bed and cradled the telephone in his lap. He could call, he thought. He could easily call. But he knew it was late, that a sudden call might disrupt whatever she and that new boyfriend of hers were doing—and if she were to answer, to be in the mood to listen, what would he say?

He held the receiver to his ear, silencing the outgoing tone with his thumb. He rehearsed: "Hello, Julie? It's me, Roger. How have you been? Good. Me? Oh, I'm up here in Big Sur and . . . well, you wouldn't believe what I'm going to do tomorrow . . . "

He stopped with a sigh, held the receiver before him and stared at it, then shook his head.

"On second thought," he spoke aloud, "it's probably best you don't know . . . "

He placed the telephone back on the nightstand and put the receiver in the cradle hard enough to make the bell toll.

CHAPTER 11

The Trip

THE BEDSIDE ALARM TRILLED. Roger could have easily slept until 7:30 a.m. and managed to arrive on site at the pre-arranged time, but he'd decided to set his clock a full hour earlier. He used much of that time to linger in bed—not to snooze, not because this was a day to be met, a day of adventure, but because he wanted some time in which to appreciate the now, the better to appreciate the changes to come.

He dressed in comfortable clothes, topping them off with his trusty bucket hat and a pair of shades, and then wandered down to the Inn's restaurant for a to-go coffee. He took his sweet time in the drinking of it, the smelling of it, and the tasting of it under the great skies of California at their most open. As he approached the bottom of the cup, the impulse to seize the day became irresistible and he wandered down the road to meet his friends.

Chuck had been the first to arrive. As he saw Frances coming down the stony path from higher ground, he cried out "Yo ho!" from his position on the beach. She was too encumbered to wave back, lugging a picnic cooler by its handle with one hand while carrying in the other the tools of dictation. Chuck dashed up the slope to give her a hand. She was appreciative. They were both dressed in cut-off jeans and cotton tops, Frances in flip-flops, Chuck in sandals; Frances' blouse was knotted in front over a black bikini top and she wore an appealing sun hat. Chuck's choice of sun shield was a black-and-white baseball cap emblazoned with the red-backed logo of STP motor oil. He found just the right spot for the cooler, nestled in the shade cast by a wall of rock near the McWay Falls.

Frances took in an appraising look around. "Where are the others?"

"Stationed at different points up and down the beach."

"Oh, I think I see some of them!" Frances waved to the specks down the jagged coastline and one of them waved back.

"They were cool about giving us some space, and having some space for themselves. Our paths may converge at some point later in the day. No obligations."

"So. Are we all set?"

Chuck patted his pocket over his heart. "Got everything we need right here."

Frances looked around, feeling suddenly dwarfed by the resplendent scenery. "It's much more beautiful down here than I expected. This is magnificent!"

"You never drove up here before?" Chuck asked, making conversation.

"I've driven through, but never stopped."

"There are advantages to slowing down, once in a while."

Frances pushed some sand with her toe. "Chuck, I was just wondering... Did you... bring any extra?"

"Franny, really? *You* want to take a trip?"

She was a trifle embarrassed. "Oh, you know, just a little one. I'd like to see what all the fuss is about."

Chuck smiled expansively. "Well, it so happens that I do have a small dose, just enough to bend your perspective a little."

"That's fine for me. A lovely little vacation."

Chuck fumbled in his pocket as Frances excitedly grabbed an iced bottle of Fresca from the cooler. By the time she'd popped the bottle cap, he had produced a sugar cube from a wrapper. He held it up to her with the smile of a jeweler. "Not the whole thing," he said. "Bite it in half. Don't chew it and swallow; let it dissolve naturally on your tongue."

Frances took another swig of Fresca, then did as Chuck directed. They smiled at one another conspiratorially, but almost immediately she registered concern. "I hope I'm not indulging my curiosity at the cost of Roger's dosage," she feared.

"Not at all," Chuck assured her. "This one is mine," he explained, popping the other half in his mouth.

"*Yours?*" She punched his shoulder. "Damn it, Chuck, you're supposed to be guiding Roger through this process! How strong is this?"

"300 micrograms, bit in half."

"Is that a lot?"

"I've gone up to 750, but it's not really something I'd do again. 300 is a good dose for Roger because he wants to go through some changes, but he also wants to stay lucid, to communicate his impressions and explore the scenery."

Roger saw the two of them in the distance, down on the beach, as he stood beside a rough-hewn, wooden observatory post near the main road. Even from this distance, the salt air, the gulls, and the sheer scenic beauty of the location were invigorating. He had made the right choice in terms of the setting.

"Ahoy!" he called down, passing through the gate.

Chuck and Frances turned and waved, trying their best to conceal their conspiratorial attitude.

"Act casual, Franny," Chuck purred, *sotto voce*. "Guides trip all the time. It's cool."

"It doesn't *feel* cool. And don't call me Franny!"

"Good morning," Roger greeted as he strolled briskly into view. "How is everyone today?"

"Ready for blast-off, Commander," reported Chuck with a snappy salute.

"We couldn't have asked for a lovelier day!" Frances enthused, putting those other feelings behind her.

Roger answered her comment with a brief, admiring look up and down the beach, then turned back to Team Corman. His cheerful smile disappeared; he was now all business. "Frances, you are ready to document?"

Frances put down her Fresca and took up her notepad and pen. "Ready."

Roger turned to Chuck: "Chuck, I trust you've come prepared?"

Chuck reached into his pocket and pulled out a square of wax paper that, unwrapped, produced a single, intact sugar cube. "Here it is, your ticket to ride. 300 micrograms."

"You feel that dosage will be sufficient."

"Not for somebody like Fonda, but it'll do for Tourist Class."

Roger accepted the cube and could see no stain on it. It was pure white on all sides. He sniffed it. There was no unusual smell. "This is to be ingested the usual way?"

Chuck snorted with amusement. "It's not a suppository, Rog."

As Roger was about to introduce it to his tongue, Chuck reached out and stopped him. He showed him something which hadn't been part of their previous preparations—a pill, dark orange in color.

"What is this?" Roger wanted to know.

"Now pay close attention, Roger," Chuck made clear, "because this—*this*—is important. This is Thorazine."

Roger nodded, then gestured to Frances to take note.

Chuck proceeded to explain: "Two important things for you to know. First and foremost, I am here with you and I'll be with you every step of the way. You can trust that absolutely. No matter what you see or think you see, I'll be your lifeline to the real world."

"I trust you," Roger said solemnly.

At this point, Chuck redirected his attention back to the little orange pill. "But, if at any point, you decide to turn back . . . if you're not enjoying the experience . . . it's within your power to cut your trip short. This pill gives you that option."

"Thorazine," Frances read back.

"Think of it as your express train from Oz back to the old farm house in Kansas. Keep it on you, someplace safe."

Roger smiled: "Very good." He accepted the pill from Chuck and put it in his right pants pocket, then glanced reflexively at his wristwatch.

"It's eight on the dot," Roger observed, smacking his lips. "I'm a little dry . . ."

Frances hopped into action. "I brought mineral water, some sodas, and your Metrecal."

"Metrecal, please. I skimped on breakfast."

"By all means, if you need to eat," Chuck advised, "eat something now, 'cause—in my experience—food will lose a lot of its appeal for you, very shortly."

Frances rooted around inside the cooler. "We have Dutch Chocolate, French Vanilla and Eggnog."

"French Vanilla."

"*Certainement, monsieur.*" Frances punctured the can and passed it to Roger.

After downing the nutritious beverage, Roger took the sugar cube—without looking at it a second time—and placed it squarely on his tongue.

"What now?" he asked, mumbling around the cube.

"Now we just wait for the party to start. It may take 20 minutes."

"I'm thinking I should have taken this back at the Inn. I would have been up and running by now. How do you suggest I make use of the time?"

"Take a walk. Look for shells. Listen to the waves. Count the clouds."

"Twenty minutes," Roger complained. "In that time, I could take a Russian space picture and turn it into something releasable."

Chuck repositioned himself directly in front of Roger and spoke to him just as directly: "Roger, I strongly recommend that you not weigh yourself down with thoughts of work. If you have to think of a Russian space picture, be the star. Fade in on the starship Big Sur. You, Roger Corman, are the cosmonaut. This coastline is the panoramic observation bay of your spacecraft. That ocean out there—the boundless seas of space. This is your adventure." He slapped his palms together like a clapper board: "Action!"

Roger rolled his eyes and walked down the beach to a cove where his nearest few friends were encamped, just to say hello. Frances watched him shrink into the distance, noting in her pad that he looked "like someone on the cusp of a great adventure."

Twenty minutes later, Frances was still sitting in the same spot, waiting for something else to happen that would require notation. Chuck was sitting nearby, hairy legs akimbo, looking greatly amused. Meanwhile, Roger, the object of his amusement, was pacing up and down the same precise measure of sand, casting fitful, petulant glances at his wristwatch.

"Twenty minutes!" he steamed. "You know what I think, Chuck? I think this 'tripping' business is a lot of nonsense. It's nothing more than the power of suggestion."

"It's coming, Roger."

"And we promised that 'Manny' of yours an associate producer's credit! How do we know this wasn't a bad batch? Did you see a stain of anything on the cube?"

"It's colorless."

Roger glanced at his watch.

"Twenty-ONE minutes! I've had it—we're leaving! This whole dingbat enterprise has cost us—cost me!—entire days of work! Work, energy, money, time . . . "

Time.

T i m e.

T i m e.

An incoming wave jostled the voyager from his reverie; he realized he hadn't consulted his watch in some time. He hadn't felt the need to do so, as its ticking had somehow receded, taking its place amid the other bric-a-brac of the seascape.

Constant sound of surf—rushing, cleansing—the breath of peace like the clinking of a hundred thousand knitting needles, those that weave reality, substance of the present, while the towering rocks rising, abounding, stood around this trilogy of cosmonauts like the remains of dead Giants, their legendary flesh dropped, cast like bark from the Redwood trees higher up to settle in the lay of the land and be pecked by gulls with a ticking sound. The steaks of these gods had ossified since those bygone days when there were no mortals around to see them, begat into rock, their mossy chest hairs reaching skyward in defeat, fallen far, fallen low over time, the slow sagging brine, left for unborn races yet to climb. Their pipe smoke still hung in the air, wafting like elegant rumors.

"Colorless?" Roger said, or thought aloud, with some astonishment. It was anything but that.

Again, he looked at his wristwatch. He watched as the minute hand zoomed ahead from 8:30 to 8:50 and back again to 7:45.

"Wait a minute . . ."

"I think we may have take-off," Chuck advised Frances as he scrambled to his feet. He rushed over to where Roger stood and squinted into his eyes. Roger looked back, mildly surprised to find his inner camera suddenly equipped with a fisheye lens.

These tall rocks, piles of fossil—fossilized fins and bone clusters, shapes of beings never before seen by comprehending eyes—the gargantua and leviathans that once thrived here—the whole earth excreted in one great shunt onto the sands of now, the plains of history. . . This thing on the ground there—it's of the earth, like me. An Earthling. Did it once speak? Is it edible? Or should I just wear it in my hair?

Roger knelt and combed the sand with a stuttering wave of his hand, his fingers leaving grooves like you see on a record album. The small living thing skittered away in shyness. His mind began to wander and he rose and followed, calmly and methodically, up the coast. It was then he first saw the castle in the distance. It was like a clearing in the ticking. He had been here many times before; how had he never noticed this? How could he never have *filmed* there? His inner location scout kicked in and he began to amble down the coastline, unfettered.

"Right beside you," Chuck assured him.

Seeing that her companions were now moving out of hearing range, Frances grabbed her notebook, took a gulp from her Fresca, and scrambled off the rock to follow.

The castle.

You're doing great, Roger. Just go with the flow.

There before him, almost close enough to touch, stood the castle with its ancestral portraits.

"Roger?"

A voice had spoken his name, but it wasn't the voice of his companions.

It was a deep voice whose tenor he knew as well as his own bones. The sound of the inrushing waves behind him pushed the heavy door open like the unseen hand of a ghost or some psychic imperative. Seamlessly, the thought took him inside. He saw an older man, sitting with folded hands in a capacious wing chair. It was his father. But at the same time, it was his grandfather and his great-grandfather. And also, the father he would someday be.

"Dad?"

His father figure spoke in his own measured cadence: "Your mother and I brought you into the world—you . . . and your brother Gene—at a time when we were feeling assured that the future, the time of your childhoods and young adulthoods, would be a time of prosperity and plenty. Then, when you were only five years old, with your years of education still before you, came the great Stock Market Crash of 1929. And, after that, the Great Depression.

"As I'm sure you remember, son, getting through those times was not easy. Not for your mother, nor for you children, nor for me. I lost my company. By the grace of God, I was able to rebuild. Whatever may come your way, you must persevere. And there is only one way to do that."

The hand of an unseen woman came to rest like a small bird upon the father's shoulder.

"Mother and I have something for you, something to help you remember our struggle, yours and ours, and the sacrifices we made together as a family."

From behind his folded hands, the father produced a wristwatch. He wound it, pressed it to his ear, then held it forward. "Do you hear that?"

Roger held the timepiece inside the shell of his ear. He listened.

Tick tick tick.

"Yes, Dad."

Then the father's voice changed to that of Vincent Price in the prologue to *Tales of Terror*:

"This is the beat of a human heart."

Each tick, he also realized, was a swing of the pendulum.

"Roger?"

—.—

Light shudders and skids, touching edges of a formation in the bible of stone, bringing recessed details of sculpture to the surface—the likeness of a hydra, a gryphon, something once washed up ashore to be hastily chronicled in dense rock that it might be recorded before decomposing under Time's boot into myth and memory—three trees yonder holding vigil... What is Time if not a pendulum? What is Time if not sand through an hourglass? Sand that is surrounding me!

"Earth to Roger, Earth to Roger. It's me, Chuck."

Chuck was on his knees in the sand beside Roger, whose head was tilted toward the ticking of his own wristwatch. Chuck and Roger had been through a lot together, always with Roger as his Captain, but now—with their roles reversed—Chuck had never seen his purposeful boss looking so lost and woebegone.

Roger looked at Chuck dolefully. He could see him perfectly well but couldn't understand why he was wearing his father's old clothes. Even so, something kicked in that he had remembered from his time as a student in Jeff Corey's acting class: If you are spoken to in character, it is necessary to reply in character.

"Yes, Dad?"

Roger's father was kneeling beside him in the sand in khaki shorts and a Hawaiian shirt. He told him straight, no pussy-footing: "Lose the watch, Roger."

"Lose it?" He didn't understand.

"Not lose it. Not literally. It won't get lost. But let me... just let me hold it for you. It's weighing you down."

Roger hesitated.

Chuck persisted, turning on the charm: "Don't you want to be free?"

Frances, standing behind Chuck, lowered herself just enough to rest her hand supportively on his shoulder, just as the hand he took to be his mother's had come to rest upon his father's shoulder a moment ago.

"I'll look after it for you, Roger," she said.

Roger slipped off the wristwatch and entrusted it to Frances. The hand that passed it over to her was that of a young boy.

With this action, the ticking faded into silence. Weightless silence.

Roger stood—feeling unburdened, liberated—and dashed toward the shoreline.

Free! The waves were skaters, racing, zephyrs of generation, sweep after sweep of them rushing in to greet, crumble, smooth out foaming in a whoosh. Cast your eyes like bread upon the waters, gray matter into Viking vessels, see in their fluctuations the oils/pigments squeezed from tubes like serpentine jewels, a painter's tools in ardent application, see and taste/taste and hear the spectacle of transparent saline hues! It's the permanent permanence of the landlocked, all these mainland metaphors. What? What's this?

Out of nowhere, Roger was nearly blind-sided by a young bicyclist. The young man was wearing a familiar ensemble of beige slacks, white shirt and blue necktie, and a burgundy cardigan. They all registered clearly as he zipped past the three of them, sand spraying high from his skidding tires.

"Hey, wait a minute!" Roger called out before sprinting after him. He sprinted all the way down the beach, where to his surprise he found the 20th Century Fox studio lot relocated. He followed the tire tracks to the old Writers' Building, where he found himself dismounting and carrying the day's mail deliveries inside. Roger was now tremulously aware, as in a dream, that he was at once the boy observed—but also the man observing, and still another presence observing them both.

This was fun!

He could feel the familiar weight and heft of the mailings—most of it correspondence, envelopes of different sizes and a parcel or two. It was here, after he had graduated from Stanford, that he got his first job as a studio messenger. He left his modest burden at the front desk. There was someone there to receive them but this vague studio employee was little more than a smudge painted on the wall. One or two envelopes fell to the floor and, as he bent over to pick them up, he noticed they were addressed to a familiar name, a man whose office was just down the marbled hall. He decided he would hand-deliver these, showing initiative.

The door he sought was the last one on the left. There was something about its placement that awakened in him an old sense of psychological dread, something whose true origin he couldn't remember. He had not only lived this, not just once but in different tenses of experience, but he had also been moved to film this, the subjective approach to a last door on the left, more than once. Apparently, no matter how many times he did this, the memory, the cause, was never exorcised.

On the door, he found the name on the envelope professionally painted on an inset beveled windowpane. He firmed his jaw, knocked on the window's wooden frame, and was told to come in. And so he did, as participant, observer, and other.

Meanwhile, Chuck and Frances were standing wind-whipped on either side of Roger, who was still knee-deep in sand but now peering into the aperture of a conch shell. Chuck was smiling wide, and Frances couldn't suppress a smile of her own at seeing them both so vulnerable and open.

The inner office was spacious: three large parallel windows, an imposing desk placed at some distance from the door, where there sat a man who shall not be named; a middle-aged producer who did not take kindly to being interrupted in the act of admiring his own manicure. One of the three windows was now filled with Roger's own gigantic face as he peered inside this dollhouse of the past, watching as the brow of his younger self knotted in confliction.

"Good morning, sir. I have your mail."

"Put it on the table there beside the door."

Roger tactfully followed the order, but chose not act on the implicit dismissal.

The producer looked up. "You got something to say, kid?"

"I don't know if you remember me, sir," he preambled, like one determined to finally and fully understand something, something which had happened but was beyond his comprehension. "I'm Roger Corman. I worked in the mail room as a studio messenger when you were still a writer here."

"Looks to me like you still do," the producer chuckled.

Roger wanted to say, in his own defense, that he had moved on, but then he realized how he was dressed, how he reached this room, how young he was at that moment. He stood there bereft of all his adult defenses.

He pushed on: "You commended me and got me promoted to script reader."

The producer laughed in spite of himself. "I did? Well, I'll be damned."

"Yes, sir. I found an overlooked script in the slush pile that I felt had considerable promise. I rewrote it and you seemed quite taken with it—remember?"

"I read a lot of scripts, kid."

"It was called *The Big Gun.*"

"*The Big Gun*?" exclaimed the producer.

"Yes, sir. I was just wondering... Has there been any... progress?"

"Well, it's called *The Gunfighter* now, kid. That was *my* addition. Well, *one* of my additions. Of course, I had to put my name on it."

"What!?"

"A name people here would recognize. Studio messengers don't write scripts, kid."

"But I was *a script reader*!"

"*Exactly!*" the producer barked, slamming the palms of his hands onto his desk. "Know your place, Ronnie!"

Roger winced.

Easy does it, Rog. Steer to the positive. Think of something that makes you happy.

"Look on the bright side!" the producer suggested, mellowing. "People say it's the best picture Greg Peck ever made. I got a pret-ty handsome bonus for salvaging that script... kicked upstairs too, as you can see... and now Mamie Van Doren is after me to produce her next picture. We're having dinner at the Polo Lounge tonight. Brother, do I have plans for her! Seriously, I owe you my thanks, kid."

Yet what was owed was obviously not forthcoming.

"But where is *my* handsome bonus?" he asked. "Where is *my* dinner with Mamie Van Doren? Where is *my* name on the script?"

"Don't you worry, kid. You're important to me—and that's why I'm gonna keep you real close. Super close! A guy in my position always needs new pages—and I want you to feed me... feed me... FEED ME!"

"I won't do it. I'm leaving!" But Roger found that more easily said than done because, suddenly, envelopes and parcels demanding to be read and evaluated had begun to proliferate in his hands and arms like the remnants of a misspent past, present, and future, overspilling his grasp to fill the office, pile up to the height of the windows, and push him outside the office and still a good distance further down the marbled hall.

Something that makes you happy, Roger. Think of the office. Think of Franny.

He was swimming in mail and, as he fought his way through the flow of it, he found the top of his desk. He was back in his office, where he could once again hear the ticking of a clock.

"I can still hear the ticking. What is that infernal ticking?" he said out loud. He stood up, rising from his swivel chair, his sand bank, and directed his question once again to the matronly temp in her 50s who was holding down his reception area.

"It's your 1:00 appointments, Mr. Corman," she explained. "The applicants for your Personal Secretary position."

The reception area, he now saw, was wall-to-wall with attractive young women—hair of every cut and style, clothes from Carnaby Street and J.C. Penney, the composed and the savvy, the buxom and the subtle, blondes, brunettes, redheads.

"Hello, ladies," he greeted them with a smile. "Send in the first, would you? We might as well get started."

When this had originally happened, it took hours. This replay was more akin to flash cards. "Why do you think you'd be right for this job?" he asked the first one.

"That's a good question," the young woman laughed. "I guess I just love movies."

Next. Why do you?

"To tell you the truth, I live less than a mile away from here. So it would be really super-convenient."

Next. Why do you?

"Mr. Corman, I can't tell you how much I need this job. I've got a little boy to feed and I can't go on leaving him with my sister. Her life is even more of a mess than mine!"

And then—look at this!—there was Frances.

There she was, inhabiting the same chair as those other women, a few years younger and dressed in somewhat more conservative clothes.

Why did she think she would be right for this job?

"Well," she chirped in her attractive Oxford accent, "I've always been impressed by your business model—economical, commercial, but nevertheless visionary—as well as your personal acumen. You have such a knack for recognizing talent and a strong record of giving it the break it deserves."

Roger accepted the compliments with an open smile. It wasn't the first time he had heard these things, but they usually came from people who were interviewing *him*.

"You probably won't remember this," she continued, "but you may recall that when you came to London to film *The Tomb of Ligeia* at Shepperton, you placed a call to Oxford University... and asked one of their tutors to send you someone who might assist you."

Roger chuckled, shaking his head in mild disbelief. "Wait a minute! I recognize you now! Frances, isn't it?"

"The same," she smiled. "I was really hoping an opportunity like this might come along someday."

"It may interest you to know... that when I called Oxford... I told them to send me their brightest critical mind. And they didn't disappoint me. Now, as I recall, you didn't type, drive or do math."

"Oh, I drive now," she said, bringing him up to date.

And that had settled that. Roger knew at that moment his mind was made up, but he was obliged to meet with the rest. What about this next one? Why did she think she was right for this position?

"What are all those creepy posters in the lobby? Did you make *those*?"

Next.

"What else can I tell you? I'm engaged to a very handsome young man from Salt Lake, who's looking forward to acing his bar exam. We're both very interested in politics. You see, in the last election, I did a lot of campaigning for Senator Goldwater!"

Flash the cards and drop them. Next. Next. Next. And then... but she wasn't there. In her absence, the sound of ticking suddenly resumed. A burning ember fell onto Roger's arm, which he rapidly brushed away, exclaiming "Hey!"

The temp in the reception area yelled out that the office was on fire.

"What? The *office* is on fire?" Roger couldn't believe it.

"I can help you out of here," someone said, maybe Julie.

"'Out of here'?" Roger didn't understand.

"Walk with me."

"Out of the office? What do you mean?"

"Just let me know if I can help."

Another ember fell, then another. Roger finally looked up in horror to see and confirm that the entire ceiling of his office was in flames, on the verge of collapsing: his office was indeed on fire, but at the same time, it was the same stock footage of the burning warehouse he had used in the incendiary climax of almost every single one of his Poe pictures. When the ceiling finally caved in, Roger was horrified to see Sam Arkoff himself, grinning gigantically down at him, tapping embers from the tip of a Churchill-sized cigar.

Roger pounded his intercom for assistance. "Help! Anybody!"

He pushed his way through the ashen framework of his office, crashing through his closed door into a skeletal reception area that ultimately delivered him back to the coastline at Big Sur, where he stood as solitary as Adam, not the first but rather the last man on earth.

The sea is the externalization of our unconscious—when man first crawled from the sea, we internalized its turmoil—everything fluid before then, just think of something to experience it, to know it, to engage it…

Once again, he saw and felt her hand cross the desk and glide into his own.

When we walked on land, we lost everything because on land we must move from here to there—we're not all one dream anymore. This California, this promised land—but isn't the real promise the vista beyond which land disappears?—perhaps to where all that is worldly disappears, leaving only endless, revolving sky—a country of the clouds. Could the sky be the sea's unconscious? What might be revealed once that becomes conscious?

Roger came to rest, lying prone upon the sand at some distance from the surf.

What composes this beach is as interesting as whom composes it. The sand—grains of time—pooling around buried stones, receding in pebbled silver—sun-dappled, surged of pure white, crowning energy possessable only in its reflection—the more real the light becomes, the more land loses definition, retreats into two dimensions and shadow—the beach is nothing but the ashen remains of cast-off wristwatches going all the way back to the first upright troglodyte. I can see it now: God was a surfer.

"How you doing, Franny?" asked Chuck, the only knob who called her that. But it wasn't bothering her.

"It's all very lovely," she half-sang, bobbing her head in rhythm to a song she'd recently heard on the radio, "Wild Thing." She wondered how it might sound were the ocean playing it and, just like that, the thing itself came in answer between her ears. She laughed to high Heaven.

From the corner of his eye, Roger roamed the fair skies whose periwinkle blue seemed to bore with determination through his concentration, which tried to find there a more teasingly variable color. He intuited that the sky, like the sea, must be teeming with life in its own way, the line separating sky from sea a mirror edge, rife with organic paramecia or whatever they were. He bided his time till his eyes could learn to see still farther, miles and miles and miles past those paisley revels to walls of azure where events of legend stood engraved, totemic, obtuse.

The higher above these waves I be, the more their great glassy flourishes become known as handwriting on the bosom of a pearl blue that skins down to pale green…

And then, out of these heavens, vasting toward him, was what at first appeared to be a magnificent bridge extending from the horizon's vanishing point, but which, under closer scrutiny, with both eyes, revealed a spectacular flotilla of ancient clipper ships. They were magnificent terrors with massive, billowing sails, emboldened by daring air, great giant breasts of breeze filling their heroic swell. As the foremost ship drew near, he could see that the sails and rigging were held in place by great lengths of the most fabulous strung jewels, that the sails themselves were weavings of such jewels. It was the saga of these ships to carry these gems to port by the chest load. Pacing the deck of the foremost vessel with captainly impatience was a haughty brunette with snow-white skin, a cartoon of a woman clad only in black stockings and heels, who leaned over the stern as it soared through the sky. He locked eyes with her somehow and she took an interest, an interest she paid out by playfully dropping opulent samples of her fabulous booty overboard—bracelets, necklaces, precious stones too large to mount.

Roger reached up and caught one of these fallen jewels. It was emerald green and wobbled in his hands like a mound of gelatin. He had never seen anything quite so beautiful, had never felt anything quite so involving. Through a surge of raw instinct, he knew what to do with it: he placed it on the ground and piled scoops of sand onto it, burying it.

There are formations here, oh yes, where a man might nestle and could tell to himself this is home, this is woman, for me and of me—scenery so arresting that no eye would wander—this is wanton, this is wife—a breeze so warm and caressing, it carries comfort, assuagement, forgiveness—a holy place, where men once came on solitary sojourns, which inspired them to build the first churches—here was real majesty—see the fronds of local flora nod their agreement, bow deep in solemn reverence. Land meets surf where flesh bonds spirit in sexual healing...

Chuck was engrossed in what was unfolding. Frances, who had retreated to a rock of her own where she could add new details to her notebook, happened to look up and tilt her head this way and that.

"Chuck? What do you think he's doing?"

Chuck wondered how to put into words what he was thinking. "He's, um, making art."

The two of them watched as Roger moved around mounds of sand with his palms, first like a man rowing, then like a man preparing to make a sand castle. What *was* he doing?

The plump jewel at rest in the palm of his hand continued to wobble. He dropped it onto the face of the sand where it was swallowed up. Then, suddenly to Roger's amazement, a bare female leg thrust up, thigh high in the most infinitesimal quartz crystals. It wrapped around him in sly invitation.

But all his friends could see was Roger suddenly dropping face-forward into the sand.

"Good God," Frances exclaimed, "has he—?"

And then—before either of them could rush to his rescue—Roger's hips began to move, to grind rhythmically against the sand.

"Oh my," Chuck chuckled. "Quite the opposite."

Roger was making a repetitive, incoherent sound, some kind of chant that begged investigation.

"I can't hear," Frances complained, her hand poised to jot down something new. "What's he mumbling?"

"Pardon me whilst I go investigate," Chuck announced. He whirled over to where Roger, um, undulated. He knelt down, close to his face. "Hey there. Everything copacetic, sire?"

Roger's face was dreamy, his cheek against the sand. "The Earth . . . is a Woman . . . and I am humping Her."

"Check." He scurried back and resumed his previous point of vantage near Frances. "You'll want to take this down," he advised.

Frances poised her Paper Mate Flair pen over the waiting page.

"He says the Earth is a Woman . . . "

". . . and I am HUMPING HER!" Roger bellowed from the beach.

Frances buried her face in her hand as Chuck toppled over, laughing.

According to Roger's lysergic thought patterns, if the Earth was a Woman, her most private of privates must therefore be the Center of the Earth, and with this insight he found himself embarking on the deepest part of his trip—a journey that not even Jules Verne could have envisioned.

Before he could say "Please," his whole humping being was taken inside Her most secret recess and he found himself plummeting, plummeting, down what appeared to be a gigantic rabbit hole. He was now in free-fall, yet plummeting slowly enough to take note of the sights encrusted in the passing subterranean walls about him. The roots of the native flora, thin near the surface, appeared to thicken as they extended further down, threading in and out of the bottomless void, assuming with the passing miles a less botanical, more mechanical aspect. Also, the deeper he fell, the closer he came to an as yet unascertainable brightness, greater than that of any natural sun.

"*What... place... is this?*" he heard Basil Rathbone ask. He saw Basil pass by, in a red smoking jacket from Western Costume, like one of the farm animals swirling around Dorothy in the eye of the tornado that took her to Oz. The thought of Oz somehow reminded him of the Thorazine tablet in his pocket. Was it getting near the time to take it? Familiar voices continued to surround and surpass him: *Do you know where you are, Bartolome?*" asked Vincent Price in *Pit and the Pendulum*. "*You are about to enter Hell. Tophet... Gehenna... Naraka... the Pit!*"

These were just two of the multitudinous images playing on countless video screens that, he could now see, lined every square inch of the earthy circumference of this rabbit hole. No, not lined—tiled. They were like the candy dots kids bought on sheets of paper. Dozens, hundreds, thousands, millions of screens, each with its own unique moving images, from the earliest Georges Méliès to the latest Lestoil commercial; but there were just as many others that were new to him, all of them wondrous in all they brought to bear on the Seventh Art. He was falling fast but he thought he even saw scenes from huge science fiction things too enormous, too rich, and too wide to be called movies—the kind of thing he might make himself if he didn't know the value of a dollar. These were displayed shoulder to shoulder with the movies he worshipped, the movies he remembered making, and also the movies he was going to make.

It occurred to him that he had somehow humped his way through to a place where there resided, as though deeply embedded in the tissues of the earth, everything ever committed to film, along with everything that would ever be committed to film in the future, all of it sequestered far below the earth's crust, all of it on equal footing—the good, the bad, the indifferent.

What powers all of this? Perhaps special rocks, stone deposits which generate magnetism, somehow harvesting and recording not only finished art but ideas in their rawest, most primal state, past present and future—somehow transmitted up to the soles of our shoes and up into our consciousness, the imperatives of where to build roads, to roll out highways, where to rest, where to eat, where to gather, where to work, where to live... where to make movies... and what to make movies about.

This was all too important to pass up. He wanted to stop and try to figure this place out. Roger—still plummeting, oncoming air combing his hair—reached out for something to hold onto, fingers searching for the cables, thick as tree roots, protruding from the soil. He grasped at them, ripping out one or two that were insufficiently anchored, causing a few screens to go black in his wake. Finally, he caught one strong enough to support him; he clutched it tight and climbed the wooden vein to a ledge that could serve as a proper foothold. He was no longer falling. He was standing erect in a place he could investigate. The ledge where he stood was the lip of a life-size screen that presented a view of the beach at Big Sur. He took a couple of tentative steps toward it and understood that this was no screen, but rather a portal.

Roger swallowed hard. He instinctively knew that this was the deepest part of his trip. He thrust his right hand deep into his trouser pocket. There in his palm was the Thorazine tablet Chuck had given to him. He reminded himself that he could take it now and all of this would disappear... or he could take those remaining steps to the full revelation of what his mind wanted to confide to him. Then, with a gesture of drama and purpose, he cast the pill away from him, allowing it to drop into those deeper levels of the void he would never see, all the way down to the earliest days of television and cinema, to ping off the surface of the first etchings of a mammoth or demon on a caveman's wall.

Roger took a deep breath and passed through the screen, somehow stepping out of the mouth of the cave at Bronson Caverns, now dressed like a romantic hero. The egress of the cave was flanked on either side by hooded figures on horseback. In the distance beyond them, though it did not match the setting geographically, was the great Keyhole Arch at Big Sur.

He looked from side to side, at the two equestrian phantoms. One of them removed her hood to reveal Miss May—the doe-eyed, brunette centerfold Roger had once admired in that month's issue of *Playboy*. Then the other followed suit, releasing a tumble of familiar blonde hair: it was Robin.

"What kind of man reads *Playboy*?" asked Miss May, provocatively.

"He doesn't read *Playboy*," Robin answered accusingly. "He reads *Variety*."

Roger was taken aback. "Ladies, you've got me all wrong!" *Tick tick tick tick*. "I read *Time*!"

He held up his wrist to prove the point, but it was bare. The two horsewomen laughed and galloped away.

In the clearing they left behind, he glimpsed a solitary female figure walking near the dunes, garbed in what appeared to be 19th century rental garments from Western Costume. Her green cloak, he imagined, probably had the name "Greer Garson" sewn into its collar. She was hooded, so he couldn't see her face, only the color of her hair—that tumble of auburn hair, now glimmering as though in Technicolor. He ran toward her in slow motion across a path of strewn flowers.

"Pardon me, Miss, but do I know you?" he asked.

"Yes, Milord."

"Then why can I not see you?"

"Perhaps it is by thy own choosing. Perhaps 'tis not the right time?"

"Then why am I seeing you now?"

"Because, Milord—this is a trailer."

Indeed, in the act of pursuing this comely phantom, he had accompanied her to a Winnebago camper on the beach, the sort of trailer used to house important cast and crew during location shooting.

Roger was confused. "I'm afraid I don't understand."

The female figure, now unmistakably Julie Halloran, spun around wielding a clapperboard inscribed with the title *The Man with Kaleidoscope Eyes*. What on Earth did that mean?

"A trailer," she emphasized. "You know—*a coming attraction!*"

She snapped the clapper shut. With its loud report, the scene suddenly exploded into a torrent of scenes from Roger's films: a giant *papier-mâché* crustacean emerged from the same cave as himself a moment ago, now raising its mighty pincers... a stout, ominous-looking man in dark glasses removed them, uncovering a bleached gaze from another planet... a giant plant yelled "Feed me!"... Beverly Garland raised her rifle, shouting "You think you're gonna make a slave of the world? I'll see you in Hell first!"

Hyperbole arced comet-like across the face of this strange conglomeration of entertainments, spelling out CRAZY, MAN... CRAZY! as the voice of a greatly amused trailer announcer promised: "Here's Roger Corman as you've never seen him before!" More hyperbole arced in the opposite direction—IT'S A GO-GO A GO-GO!—over jerky, 16mm color shots of Vietnam, a field of high grass with grunts scurrying. "Yes, that movie-a-minute madcap is at it again... and it's all happening in COLORSCOPE in *'The Man with Kaleidoscope Eyes'*!"

Roger himself was now laughing, grasping the absurdity of this bombardment. He put on his shades to shield his eyes, fearing that the overload of entertainment, of information, of insight, might blind him, would blind him, had blinded him, but he could instantly see that the kaleidoscopic energy was not pressing upon him from without, but rather shining out from within.

"Of course! Of course!" he repeated, smiling.

With a brisk jerk, he reached up and removed his shades from twin spinning pools of dizzying, kaleidoscopic color...

At some point during Roger's trip, Chuck and Frances had followed him up to higher ground, up among the Redwoods. Though he was not particularly aware, it was actually there that the greater portion of his trip had taken place. For hallucinated reasons neither of them was able to penetrate given their own unmoored states of mind, Roger had chosen not to use one of the provided paths to scale the hillside, but rather climbed upwards by grappling a cluster of deep roots bursting through the sand and rock.

There was silence. Calm. A gentle breeze.

Roger was curled up at the foot of a colossal tree. Frances was perched nearby on a slab of driftwood. Chuck was stretched out on the grass. He caught her gazing at Roger with a tender smile, appreciative of the look of rest and refuge on his face.

"You kinda like your boss, don't you, Franny?"

"Of course I like him," she said. "He's a brilliant man. A brilliant, vexing man."

"The worst kind."

"Yes," she agreed. "And the best."

They let those words set a tone for the next minute or so, until Frances broke the silence with another word. "Frankie."

"Beg pardon?" asked Chuck.

"My friends call me Frankie. Those I let."

"Duly noted. So why haven't I ever heard Roger call you. . . ?"

"We work together so well," she explained, cutting off the question. "I think we both know it wouldn't serve either of us to bollox things up. Look at him. I've never seen him so . . . contented. Bloody restless man."

"And how are *you* doing? Enjoying your little 'vacation'?"

"Yes, very much. It's been lovely. Very peaceful. Something I can rarely say around Roger."

As Frances spoke his name, Roger began to stir in his fetal position in the veiny lap of the great Redwood.

"Heads up," Chuck alerted Frances. "He might be coming down. Time?"

Frances consulted Roger's wristwatch: "1:33."

"We started at eight sharp. That's what, under six hours? I'll be damned. Ahead of schedule."

"He'll like that," she smiled.

Suddenly, Roger sat bolt upright. He looked agitated, excited. He tried to speak but wasn't quite able to form whole words—or, once words were mastered, full sentences. His speech was slightly slurred and his tongue, sticky, smacked and smecked. It angered him because he had snapped out of whatever he had been snapped into with news of tremendous urgency.

Chuck opened a canteen and passed it to Roger. "Take it easy, man. Rehydrate." Roger gulped from the container. "Slow," Chuck advised sternly.

After a minute or so of slow gulping, Roger began to remaster his powers of speech and a modicum of calm. It was cooler here, under these towering leaves, away from direct sun; he felt sheltered as well as connected. Simply by resting his temple against the ancient bark of this tree, he felt a connection to the place from which he'd just been delivered. These trees, he knew in his very bones, were the first antennae.

"Take this down, Frances," Roger instructed. "We mustn't lose any of this in–, in–..."

"Insight?"

"In-*formation*," he corrected her sternly.

"I'm right with you," she said, pen poised.

"Have you ever wondered why, whenever we lay down, we slip into the world of dreams? I found the answer. Anything anyone has ever thought, ever dreamed, ever imagined, ever turned into a story or a book or a movie or a television series—it's all down there, at the center of the earth, in a vast subterranean reservoir of information! Don't stare at me, write this down! I'm not sure how it all got down there in the first place. Visitors from elsewhere, possibly. But the receptors are in place and whatever is transmitted through the air, our conversations, our ideas, our dreams, at any given moment, is picked up here"—he said, slapping the trunk of the Redwood—"by these receptors and transmitted down there by these..."—he kneeled back down to caress one of its gigantic roots—"these cables, which we presume to call roots. They lead down there to a vast netherworld of subterranean vaults, and in these vaults resides everything ever committed to film! And everything *never* committed to film! And everything that will ever be committed to film! But... how could that be?"

Frances, who didn't have time to write any of this down, looked dumbly at Roger.

Chuck laughed through his nose: "Best. Trip. Ever."

"Don't laugh at me! You, of all people, should recognize the importance of this! Don't you see, Chuck? This can be tapped into! Once upon a time, people came to this state from all over the world to pan for gold, but I've found something infinitely more precious than gold, because what do people do with gold? They produce movies! I found the mother-lode down there—I *own* it! My God, I've discovered a new art form!"

"Rog," Chuck tried to reason with him. "You were just trippin' balls. I'm not saying that what you experienced doesn't *mean* something, but it sure as hell ain't real—whatever 'real' means."

Roger turned to Frances. "Movie theaters as we know them will have to be completely redesigned. Those that exist now will be useless. We'll need to tear out the seats so that moviegoers can go in and lie down, closer to the ground, because that's the only way to access the signals. You just lie down on the ground," he explained, while demonstrating, "and . . . This is going to completely remove the middle man; it's going to totally eradicate the cost of print duplication and distribution!"

"And the need for filmmakers, too," Chuck observed.

Roger sat up and shot him a look. "You're just a jealous guru," he said. "After all these years of searching, I reach this place of wisdom and you just want to shut it down. I have to pee."

Left alone momentarily, Chuck and Frances exchanged bemused looks.

"I do acid and I watch my skull melt," Chuck philosophized. "He drops acid and discovers underground movies."

A few hours later, the three of them loaded their gear back into Roger's Mercedes and Chuck's trailer. They joined their fellow travelers for an early dinner at the Inn's restaurant and compared notes on their various experiences. There were one or two other trippers in the caravan, but most had come simply to dwell within that scenery and to feel its peace.

"Say, Rog," Chuck said, swallowing a spoonful of ice cream sundae, "there was one point in your trip when you said something I didn't understand."

"Oh?"

"When you were climbing up here to the Redwoods from the beach, at one point, you said '*I can still see!*'"

"No, he didn't," Frances objected.

"Yeah, he did."

Chuck very much disagreed, but he thought it best to let the subject drop.

"I don't remember," Roger admitted. "Did you succeed in recording all the essentials, Frances?"

"To the letter!" she replied proudly. She would later open her pad to bask in her accomplishment and was taken aback to discover, after a point, page after page of weird little scribbles and drawings of flowers and vines.

"Well," Roger announced, "shall we get started, heading back?"

"At our own chosen speed," Chuck agreed.

Frances asked her companions if she ought to do the driving, and Roger was grateful for the suggestion. She and Chuck piled into the car as Roger lingered behind for a moment, to drink in the beauty of the site one last time through eyes of renewed wonder.

You can see up the coastline a good 20 miles—all the way to another life looking back at you.

Roger placed his hand on his heart and felt its strong beating. The auburn-haired woman in the green hood flashed through his mind—the books he'd read had mentioned there would probably be occasions of this, "flashbacks" as they were cinematically known. There was a sense he couldn't quite shake, of having not yet fulfilled his mission here. He started back to the car, but turned on his heel and looked here, there, and everywhere for clues as to what might remain undone. The image of the Keyhole Arch provided the answer. He remembered filming Jack Nicholson there, a couple of years earlier, in the opening scene of *The Terror*. He rode his horse into frame and sat uncomfortably on its saddle. The take didn't amount to anything, so Roger called for a second one.

"What do I do, Roger?" Jack had whined. "I feel kinda stupid just sitting here. I know it's for effect, but what is the goddamn effect?"

Roger had ransacked his brain for an answer, but really, it wasn't his job. He told Jack as much, reminding him that he was playing a soldier in Napoleon's Army. What would such a man be thinking as he arrived here, at a place of peace after so much turmoil, with no immediate obligations, understanding for the first time in his adult life what it meant to be his own man, free after years of service, looking forward to seeing once again the woman he once loved—and lost?

Jack answered simply by nodding that he was ready for the take. Roger, Floyd his cameraman, the whole crew leaned forward to see what would happen when "Action!" was called. What happened was this: Jack rode the horse once again into frame, foregrounding the Keyhole Arch. He looked beaten and world-weary. He reached inside his cape to the watch fob in his vest pocket. He consulted the time. Then, with a yank, he disengaged the watch from its chain and cast it to the ground. Never again did he need to know what time it was. Brilliant—and Floyd insisted on a whole extra set-up to show the waves coming in and swallowing it up.

That was it. Roger followed his impulse: he unfastened the watch from his wrist—held it up to watch the lowering sun dazzle the face of it one last time—and let it fall to the ground at the edge of a patch of wildflowers.

He then strode purposefully back to his car, dropped amiably into the shotgun seat, and said "Let's go home."

The three friends made their way back to Los Angeles without speaking much. Each was closeted in their own subjective recollections of the day. As Roger's thoughts moved from one thing to another, sometimes taken off himself by sights passing by outside the car, he occasionally felt lysergic ripples passing through his body, not unlike the way he sometimes felt spectral waves carried through his body after hours spent in the ocean; these, however, played hob with his senses of reality. There were times when he thought back to his subterranean adventure and understood that it had been less actual than analogy; then the waves would reshuffle his biological makeup and doubt once again became conviction. Such things could be both.

About a half- hour into the drive home, it became clear that none of the three was in a mood to talk. Frances intuited that Roger and Chuck were processing the day, regathering themselves, as indeed she was. She instinctively punched in a radio station servicing the area and found the disc jockey taking on-air requests. The DJ was a woman who spoke in a relaxed, easy-going, conversational manner, not like the male motormouths abounding on AM channels, for which they were all silently thankful. The DJ was speaking on the phone to a girl named Tina who wanted to hear "Love Is All Around" by The Troggs.

It began with just the plucked vibrations of an electric bass. It was a naked heartbeat sound with a mild resonance around it, as if it was being sounded in a cavern or someplace deep underground that a Trogg might inhabit. Once the bass had stated its opening pattern, a graceful, chiming electric guitar figure gentled against it, aligned with it, adding flesh to the skeleton. To his surprise, Roger felt on the edge of his seat. He reflected on his free-fall to the center of the earth and all that he seen and heard down there, and the primitivism of this song called to him like an echo from a place that bore only his own footprint. He listened intently to the words, to the postponed introduction of the high hat and classical string accompaniment and felt the music reaching into him, into his chest.

What was happening to him? Why were these rough emotions overtaking him with each musical development, each verse? Was it because of what the lyric was saying, or was it the way the spare and simple instrumentation underscored those words?

He watched the scenery passing him by as Frances piloted them back to Los Angeles, each new sight seeming to disappear as soon as it presented itself, but there was no worry, no despair, for he knew there was no beginning, there was no end. Even when the song ended, it seemed to continue. And so indeed change had come, and this was only the first of the many ways in which the change he craved would manifest.

He was glad he wasn't driving. He kept his head turned toward the window, to hide his brimming eyes from the others. He was uncomfortable being seen when he was feeling so good. Was all music going to affect him this way now, or was it just this one song?

Several hours later, having seen Frances and Chuck safely back to the office and their respective cars, Roger motored home in solitude. He entered his house feeling justified—and exhausted. He dropped his bags inside the front door, looking like a man returned from a great adventure, drained but content. He collapsed onto his sofa, from which vantage he surveyed the room with tired, acid-dried eyes—he looked at his belongings, his mementos. He saw his tennis rackets, the clipper ship in the bottle, the pictures on the walls, the books. Everything was where it had been left—but something was now out of place.

Was it him? No, it wasn't him.

He sat upright, the better to assess the problem. He found it immediately. With abrupt determination, he crossed the room to the framed poster for *Day the World Ended.* He had always considered this 1955 picture—a film obviously about the end of the world as we know it—to be his first truly self-expressive work, the first of his many movies to really represent him.

Now, it no longer did. This day, today, was the day his world—his way of looking at the world—really ended.

He took the poster down, leaning it against the wall with its dynamic Albert Kallis artwork facing away from view.

Then he stared deeply, profoundly, approvingly at the nail left nakedly exposed on the wall.

What would hang there next?

"Not the end," he vowed. "The Beginning."

CHAPTER 12

October 1966 (slight return)

THE MERCEDES' HEADLIGHTS blazed through the dawn's early light. Roger's shoes crunched over the detritus in the dirt road. A flashlight led him through the particulars.

The watch was still there.

He wiped the dew from its face onto his shirt's sleeve and strapped it back onto his wrist. Then he drove back home, where he slept straight through the next two days.

CHAPTER 13

NOVEMBER 1966—JANUARY 1967

THE REMAINDER OF ROGER'S YEAR would be spent in preparation for *The Trip*—which was shaping up to be his most ambitious film, and his most personal since *The Intruder*. In order to meet the August openings that American International had already booked, pre-production would likely resume after the year-end holidays, with filming commencing in late January, early February.

The weeks immediately following Roger's trip were a bit wobbly as they required him to start concerning himself with the earliest aspects of pre-production while, at the same time, taking frequent itineraries of his internal changes. He sometimes likened his self-image in these days to a plastic hobby kit, taken apart and reassembled in ways invisible to the naked eye but absolutely apparent as enhancing to his innermost self. There were new levels of himself that he took into meetings, into editing rooms, into dates, into his cars as he drove home late at night, alone.

The books he had read on the subject of LSD had prepared him to anticipate the phenomena of "acid flashbacks"—instances wherein he would find himself temporarily back in the sway of how things looked and felt and seemed in the depths of his trip. True enough, such lysergic reassertions did persist, though in a non-aggressive, even companionable way. There were moments when he might focus on some image or emotion sent back to him from the apex or nadir of his experience and feel it locking into some otherwise inaccessible part of his brain, actualizing it and making him feel that he was now more than he was. Whenever this happened, he imagined the human brain must be full of such junctures and that, if we could only identify and somehow provide the correct inputs, the human animal might become capable of many talents thought to be impossible, such as instantaneous computation, prophecy, even flight. Without exception, these awakened connections quickly resumed their usual dormancy, unable to be re-accessed through the paths of concentration. He came to think of them as little postcards from Big Sur saying, in a variety of ways, "Wish You Were Here."

Both Jack and Peter had been eager to hear what went down at Big Sur and paid a joint visit to his office, where Roger held court with anecdotes and his ever-present can of Metrecal. Everyone who listened to Roger's account agreed it was one of the best they had ever heard described, especially the part about the clipper ship strewn with babes and jewels. Some—Peter in particular—noted how fortunate Roger was to have navigated a clear path through any hint of negativity. Sure, Roger had encountered a few dark moments during his trip but they were all thresholds to resolve, deliverance, metamorphosis. Jack was a little less forthcoming about his own personal details, but Peter was frank about the darkness he frequently encountered during his trips, because his lot had been to experience and process a great deal of pain. He had sought to master it by being prolific in his adventuring and casting wide in matters of dosage, and somehow his trips and his approach to life were becoming happier. Roger wasn't like his actor friends in this regard; he was almost always calm and smiling, even on film sets when faced with problems of time or money. Roger one day realized that, having now taken an actual trip, he was poised to direct a new film called *The Trip*—and a corridor of mirrors opened up. This gave him the insight to understand his past experiences of filmmaking as *faux*-trips of a sort, wherein he would stand inside enclosures of artificial scenery with costumed actors, whom he would guide through fantasies of travel and romance, mystery and nightmare. The movies he had made in the past might very well have purged him of any darkness that might otherwise have been invoked by the chemical in his sugar cube.

Now that he stood on the other side of this experience, Roger had the expectation that taking LSD might become something he would continue to do, now and again. His first trip had shown him previously undisclosed aspects of himself as he was before acid; now he wanted to subject the Roger he was after acid to the same merciless lens. To now be able to say he'd taken the drug, that he was "experienced," changed his own definition of himself, made him seem less of a square in the midst of a very hip group of people, and he imagined that LSD might go on to become a regular part of his daily life—not unlike Metrecal. He didn't know exactly what kind of LSD Chuck had procured for him, plain French Vanilla he supposed, but he'd since heard there were many different kinds—Orange Sunshine, Blue Cheer, Owsley Purple, Windowpane—and he thought it would be educational, even fun, to meet and converse with all the available colors of himself.

Somehow, it never happened.

Leary's book made it clear that the ideal setting for pursuing this introspection was in the company of trusted friends, and Roger's workaholic tendencies kept that group narrowed to a select few close colleagues. He understood that further tripping under Frances' supervision would be professionally inappropriate, as indeed it would be to expose himself over-frankly, over-candidly, ass over teakettle to Chuck or even Jack; it was essential to their continued collaboration that he maintain a modicum of executive distance. It never occurred to him to call Robin, Marsha, or any of the other women he'd been seeing recently; they might have been willing enough to sign up for the program, but it was too easy to imagine himself becoming absorbed in self-examination and bonded to them as a result. He continued to think back to Julie Halloran, but he didn't yet consider himself to be the man he needed—no, wanted—to be before resuming contact with her. He was also concerned that, if she knew he was experimenting with LSD, literally breaking the law out of self-interest, it might give her the wrong idea about his personal character. The Roger that she knew, however slightly as a result of their chemistry, their job interview, and the few dates that followed—this became the Roger to which he found himself aspiring, and may offer the best explanation of why a second trip never happened.

Unless you count the movie which resulted.

—.—

Roger got his first actual foretaste of the film in a large envelope sent to his offices from Sam and Jim, containing copies of AIP's annual booklet announcing the company's exciting new titles for 1967. Thrillingly, *The Trip* was posited front and center. Roger never quite lost his sense of wonder in regard to this aspect of the process; he had yet to shoot so much as a foot of film, yet somehow the promotional art generated by AIP's art department conveyed a sense of having been created in direct response to the completed product.

The campaign for *The Trip* was like nothing Roger had ever seen before. It featured an attractive female face, haloed in blonde hair, looking up in chimerical bewilderment at superimposed images of a—perhaps even her own—(not quite) nude body, suspended in free-fall. The hyperbolic text didn't suggest a story, instead provocatively offering LSD as an anagram for "a Lovely Sort of Death." It was spookier than he might have liked, nevertheless undeniably effective in its baiting of the general public. The artwork made Roger eager to make the picture it represented, though the fine print underscored a major problem yet to be solved.

This fine print read "Starring PETER FONDA and FEMALE STAR"—Roger had yet to cast any women in the picture. By definition, the film was going to be the story of a man's inner journey; by design, it didn't have much to offer actresses of substantial reputation. Basically, there were three female roles: 1) Sally Groves, Paul's wife, his bittersweet partner in a failing marriage; there was 2) Glenn, a woman whom Paul discovers on the fringes of the counterculture, who is really into people on acid because she thinks they're "beautiful"; and lastly there was 3) Flo, a stranger whom Paul encounters at a public laundromat during his trip, a woman who has advanced into middle age without finding love, who has given up on her chances to the extent of wearing curlers in public, and who has retreated behind unbecoming sweatshirts and a wall of sarcasm.

Of the three parts, Flo was by far the meatiest, though written for a character actress somewhat past her bloom; it was a role Roger had automatically reserved for his friend Barboura Morris, known since his acting class days, whom he'd cast in *A Bucket of Blood* and a few other features during her ingénue years in the 1950s. He'd just given her a small role in *The Wild Angels* and she'd done well and appreciated the chance to work.

In contrast, Sally had only one brief dialogue scene, followed by various almost anonymous sex scenes under bombardments of psychedelic lighting; it was a one- or two-day job at best, hardly likely to attract much except possible pictorial coverage in the pages of *Playboy*.

Glenn was a somewhat more substantial role, in that she had more than a single dialogue scene, yet was inescapably secondary. All things told, the script was helplessly guilty of not having enough for actresses to do while, at the same time, asking too much of them. Roger had been around the block often enough to know that someone always came along to play those parts; usually the results were acceptable, once in a blue moon they might even be magical, but it was the sort of problem that could be trusted to solve itself.

The male roles, for some reason, were always easier to fill. Of course, Peter Fonda was already committed to the project, and they had also received confirmation of Dennis Hopper's interest in playing the role of Max. Another actor Roger was keen to involve was Bruce Dern, who had been excellent as Loser in *The Wild Angels* and had been placed under contract to AIP for another two pictures. Though the real-life Bruce was a health nut and pretty much a straight arrow, he seemed the obvious choice to play John, the psychedelics guru who would serve as Peter Fonda's guide in *The Trip*.

Roger had the script messengered to Bruce, along with word that Peter Fonda would once again be playing the lead, and an appointment was made to coincide with the actor's afternoon run. He arrived on time, looking tanned against the whites of his shirt, shorts and running shoes, his *Wild Angels* scruffiness having now achieved a sort of leonine splendor. The combination of his racing heart and ruddy highlights made his dark brown eyes look particularly soulful, searching, and candid. Roger couldn't imagine John looking any other way.

"Thanks for coming down," Roger greeted him, shaking his strong, damp hand. "Can I offer you . . . a towel or something?"

"Sure, if you got one," Dern smiled boyishly. Whenever Dern smiled, his face—that of a beatific poet—all but bloomed in a beguiling spread of horse teeth and a scrunch of his eyes; onscreen, it was his secret weapon.

"Frances? A towel for Bruce?" Roger called into the outer reception area. "Go on, take a seat."

"Really?" he asked, initially hesitant to soil one. Then he admitted "You don't have to tell me twice," before dropping into one of the chairs facing Roger's desk.

Frances came in with cold refreshments and an apology. "No towel, I'm afraid, but I found these napkins."

Bruce thanked her with humor and charm and began patting himself down with them as she left the room, closing the door discreetly behind her.

"Bruce," Roger began, "I assume you've had a chance to read the script, and I'd like to start by saying I hope you're interested in playing the part."

Dern refreshed himself with two or three gulps of ice water. "Well," he began after a satisfied swallow, "sure, I mean it's not the usual psycho guy people want me to play. But gee, I dunno, Rog . . . "

"Is it an availability problem?"

"Oh no," he insisted, "no siree. It's a few things, really. First, I gotta tell you, this guy would be a reach for me—which I appreciate—but I'm not sure I'd be the right guy."

"Oh?"

"I mean, wouldn't Jack be better for that part? I mean, he's the guru, it being his script and all."

"Unfortunately, Jack's going to be tied up making a new picture."

"Oh, yeah? What's it called?"

"*Hell's Angels on Wheels,*" Roger confided, unhappily. "That is neither here nor there, really. It's Jack's script, but I never saw him in this role. The role of John needs you. I want that authority you showed in *The Wild Angels*. You had such a calm, grounded presence."

"Of course I was calm and grounded, Roger! I was playing a dead guy!"

"Which is harder than it looks, don't think I don't know," Roger schmoozed. "Any other concerns?"

"Well, my other concern is with this LSD, Roger. John knows all about it, but I don't know the first thing about it. You took some, right? So what is it? I mean, what the hell is it?"

"You don't know?"

"Hell, no. I'm not part of that dope scene. Give me a Coke and a powdered donut and I'm a happy man."

"It's not really dope. It's not escapist by definition."

"But it's an illegal drug, right?"

"It was actually legal until fairly recently—and so far, it's illegal only in California and Nevada."

"So, if it's not escapist, what is the attraction of this stuff?"

Roger moved aside some of the clutter on the right corner of his desk, then walked around and sat there, where he could communicate with Bruce more directly and intimately.

"Bruce, it's a drug in the nature of a tool," he tried to explain. "It holds up a mirror of sorts to the user, to the planes of his thinking. It's not escapist. It's more confrontational."

Dern looked confused.

So Roger pressed on: "Let me see if I can give you an example of its power. In my own experience of L . . . S . . . D, I spent most of the day lying face down on the ground!"

Dern all but bit his lower lip, trying not to smile. "Okay," he allowed, cagily.

Roger understood that he was being humored. This wasn't quite the summation his jury of Rogers had hoped for. "I wasn't unconscious," he explained. "I was the opposite of unconscious. In full and utter consciousness, I took a journey to the center of the earth!"

"I didn't see that in the script."

"No, it's not in the script. I'm telling you *my* story."

"But ain't nothin' down there, Roger."

"Ohhhhh yes, there is!" Just thinking about it again made Roger actually chortle.

"I mean, aside from rocks and dirt and shit. What did you find down there?"

"Bruce, I found a vast subterranean library, whose holdings ranged from the Alpha through the Omega of filmed entertainment. I saw countless screens of information, embedded in the rock below. They were all illuminated and running, showing every story ever told in endless loops, every story that will *ever* be told!"

Roger paused for effect. Bruce looked at him, waiting for the story to continue.

"They're all down there—the movies already made, but also the movies that never got made and the ones still waiting to be made, and they're flickering away down there like the ore of the next gold rush, waiting for the right mediator to figure out a way of bringing them up, or transmitting them up to the surface!"

"Underground movies," Bruce said, with a slight smile. "That's pretty funny, Roger."

"Why does everyone keep *saying* that?" Roger stood up, indignant. "Am I making any sense to you at all?"

Bruce stood up as well: "Of course. If Peter takes this shit and starts seeing animals climbing out of his wallpaper, he's gonna need a combination shrink, priest, and crossing guard. I'm your man."

Roger walked Bruce to the door. Halfway out the door, and Roger already halfway back to his office, Bruce poked his head back inside to ask, "Can I keep the beard? My wife kinda likes it."

"I insist," Roger smiled back. "It radiates wisdom."

Finding and securing filming locations was in some ways the most challenging conundrum. Roger firmly intended *The Trip* to perpetuate his shifting away from the earlier set-bound Poe pictures toward more realistic settings and exteriors, as initiated with *The Wild Angels.* Two principal locations had to be found: the home of Paul's acid guru John, and the sprawling pad/compound of the drug dealer Max. The guru's house needed to be as *au courant* as possible, not only beautiful but innovative in its design—and, most importantly, accessible to beautiful natural scenery. This tall order was eventually filled to perfection by an L-shaped property at 1309 Davies Drive in Beverly Hills, originally built in the 1930s by the Woolworth's heiress for her son. Its current resident was

Arthur Lee, lead singer of the racially integrated rock group Love, who had sublet it from its current owner. Arthur's wild tastes in decoration meant the space hardly needed redressing—it was a ready-made combination aerie/menagerie of psychedelia, boasting a spectacular panoramic view of the city below and a heated indoor/outdoor pool as befit someone with a recording contract for Elektra Records.

Frances succeeded in tracking down Max's spacious lair—whose main requirement was that it look like a fortress yet project a "welcome all" sensibility—by reasoning that fact must have already found its way to whatever spot fiction was seeking. She spent a night or two hitting the clubs up and down the Strip, striking up casual conversations with various longhairs, and quizzing them about whether there were any scoring points about town. As fate would have it, there was indeed a mansion known as "The Psychedelic Temple" at 1039 S. Ardmore Avenue, previously known as the San Souci Culture Temple—and before that, the former home to silent screen legend Rudolph Valentino. It was marvelously spacious, containing a huge, empty dance floor with a checkerboard floor and a circular mezzanine above. It was simply made for a 360-degree shot of a joint being passed around the central crash area.

The script also included a suspenseful yet amusing sequence in which Paul, its tripping protagonist—having lost track of his guide and taken to the streets—breaks into a suburban family home and makes Frankenstein-like friends with a little girl. Along with her husband Harry Bernsen, actress Jeanne Cooper (another acting class alumnus from Roger's Coke and cheeseburger days, whom he'd cast in his 1957 quickie *Rock All Night*) offered their house to the production, and also made a successful pitch for their daughter Caren to play the little girl. At the end of the film, a beautiful seaside house was needed for the trysting spot of Paul and his gorgeous blonde acquaintance Glenn; this one fell into Roger's lap one afternoon as he was making conversation with a tennis opponent at his health club. Arrangements were also made to film a couple of scenes at The Bead Game, where—once upon a time—Roger had celebrated the success of *The Wild Angels* with its warring scribes.

The company became so preoccupied with finding and securing suitable interiors that, in the end, they had no time to scout original exteriors. They had to simply go with those areas already familiar to Roger and his crew. These included Bronson Canyon (the home and harbor to numerous Roger Corman alien invasions), the Sunset Strip, and of course, Big Sur, but—because filming there would have to be limited (i.e., shot *guerilla*-like without the usual legal permits)—the beach shots would probably need filling in with those shots similarly grabbed at Leo Carrillo State Beach (rallying spot for all of Sam & Jim's *Beach Party* pictures) and different points along Malibu.

"It's not going to match," Frances pointed out.

"Frances," Roger sighed resignedly, "it's *The Trip*. It doesn't really have to match."

It was now the Friday before the start of filming. The production office was a riot of activity. The central soundstage was literally framed by narrow corridors lined with offices and dressing rooms. Young people, many of them interns sent over from UCLA, were running errands and carrying messages back and forth among the various departments; racks of fringed or pin-striped clothing from J.C. Penney were being pushed along on casters; gofers carried cups of coffee; occasionally someone with real initiative might show up, excitedly waving a prop or piece of set dressing they thought the show couldn't do without. There was a feel underlying this hubbub which spoke of shared purpose, creative expression, and libido—it was very much the vibe of a co-ed college dorm. Everyone understood they were there to work, to work hard and hopefully advance; this green-lit, gypsy jubilance was the only reason anyone ever aspired to the film business. The giddiness was addicting, the intimacy unavoidable, and it got a number of the people you never hear about laid.

Hung in the midst of the busiest corridor—the one where the publicity department, makeup room and director's office could be found—was a bulletin board adorned with Monday's call sheet, clippings of inspirational art (everything from hand gestures as depicted in ancient Orthodox iconography to R. Crumb), and personal messages ranging from requests for places to crash to needs for lifts.

At the moment, Bonnie Prendergast—the script supervisor on the picture—was sitting down in a large room designated for wardrobe at General Studios, running lines with Angelo, a gruff-voiced dwarf actor, as he was receiving adjustments on his medieval costume. "Who knows what reality or any of that is?" she read from the page before her.

Angelo puffed up a cloud of acrid smoke from a cheap White Owl cigar. "Vietnam . . . auto safety," came his gruff, if highly pitched, voice in response.

"Look again."

Jack Nicholson was hovering outside the open door, leaning against the wall and grinning from ear to ear. He was nervous about intruding, but keenly interested in watching the spectacle of his kaleidoscopic vision coming together and taking shape. Possibly also in the back of his mind was that he might have a shot with Bonnie if he hung around the place long enough.

Jack had seen Roger on the premises, but only in small isolated bursts of beleaguered unavailability—like right now, as he and Frances swept by, taking a turn toward Stage B. Everyone on the crew had questions and Roger needed to have a ready answer for each and every one of them, an answer which might have to be off the cuff but for which he must ultimately take full responsibility. Jack could afford to wait to talk to him; it's not like much of anything else was going on in his life.

As Roger and Frances turned the corner, Frances split off from him and grabbed the black receiver from a wall phone. It was bordered by posted messages. She dialed a number and waited to connect. Then, a few beats later, she spoke:

"Peter? It's Frances Doel. Thank you—yes! He's *still* buzzing! Look, I'm calling because Roger needs you to come in to review wardrobe. We need to set up a time. No, we start shooting next week—we need you here *this afternoon!* Yes, that's right . . . You have some things that might work? Bring them with you, by all means . . . I think he wants to give you his sweater, the red one. It's a cardigan; he wore it up at . . . that's right." As she spoke, she looked at the posted messages on the board and took down one or two she considered unsuitable for production morale.

Some members of the construction crew were hammering nails into planks of wood, the sound bouncing from the broad walls and high ceilings of the soundstage. Others were covering the walls of a room within the space with colored cellophane, dangling streamers, images of Kennedy, Che Guevara, Bob Dylan, the shooting of Nguyễn Văn Lém—some of them specifically mentioned in Nicholson's script. A rickety-looking merry-go-round, festooned with ribbons of crepe and tinsel, was positioned somewhat lopsidedly near the center of the space, looking as though it had been dropped there from a great height.

Roger wandered in, coffee in hand, looking over the schedule his production manager had submitted to him. It broke the filming of the $450,000 project down to his favored three weeks of production: one week in the studio, one week on various locations, and one week for loose ends and special effects photography. It was workable.

As the lights on the carousel flared up, Roger looked up from the papers at hand and saw a shadowy figure lurking there in stone-washed jeans, cowboy boots, and a white Stetson. He had been trying to mount one of the carousel horses—not a simple matter given the dumpy, unstable aspect of the prop—and as the lights came up, he staggered backwards, asking the Infinite, "Whoa! Did I do that?"

Roger started walking across the studio floor toward the man, who somehow looked perfectly natural once he sat astride the wooden pony. It was only then that he recognized Dennis Hopper—not an expected visitor on this particular day, but welcome nonetheless.

"Dennis!" Roger exclaimed in greeting. "I'm Roger Corman." They shook hands. "Thank you for coming down. I wasn't expecting you today—things are a little crazy here at the moment—but it's great to finally meet you. I'm so glad you've agreed to be part of our picture."

"Oh, absolutely my pleasure, man. Anything for Jack, right? I mean, he's some kinda friggin' genius, man. Did you read his script?"

"I did. I commissioned it. I'm directing it."

Dennis reacted as though a flaming meteor of common sense took a diagonal pass through the soundstage. "Oh, right! Of course you did! This is all your doing! This is like your trip, man!"

As Dennis reeled, his stature in the saddle slowly tipped sideways to an angle closer to 45 degrees.

"Careful there," Roger said, catching him and helping him to straighten himself.

"Totally cool, man," Hopper replied amiably. "Here, let me get offa this… high horse and get down there, where you are. Eye to eye, like."

He slid off the pony and the two men took a seat, side-by-side, along the curving black-painted edge of the carousel.

"Do you smell paint?" Hopper asked. "We're not sitting on, like, wet paint, are we?"

"I don't think so, but some painting was underway here earlier today."

Hopper cut loose with a raucous laugh. "Maybe it's *Old* Paint I'm smellin'," he laughed, pointing to the lacquered wooden horse with its flaring nostrils. "Anyway, man, so this part you want me to play… Max. I read the script and I see him a certain way, right? But I need to see how you see him. I want to please my director—and argue with him, if I have to."

"Okay," Roger smiled.

"Now in the early part, he's a kind of drug dealer, right? But he's also a kind of shepherd among these lost souls of the street. He finds people, he cares for them, he puts them on what they need because—bottom line, right?—the cat's a capitalist at heart. I know this guy. Fuck, I've been this guy! But what I don't get is the Max who appears in Paul's dream, the Judge who presides over this merry-go-round."

"You've read the whole script? Or just your pages?"

"The whole script, man. I'm a responsible actor. I read it the night I got back home from up in Lodi. I was making a movie with Paul Newman and, let me tell ya, they've got some pretty groovy ideas up there about how to wash cars!—but I don't, I don't… I don't remember any merry-go-round."

"You remember the courtroom?" Roger asked directly.

"Oh, yeah. The courtroom I remember."

"This is the courtroom," Roger explained. "Of course, it's a trip, so…"

"So it doesn't *look like* a courtroom," Hopper understood. "It looks like what a courtroom *really* is."

"Jack's idea," Roger admitted. "I'm trusting him. I'm not sure it will work."

"It will, man," Hopper assured him fervently. "It's gonna work like gangbusters. Okay, man—tell me how you see Max."

"First of all, Dennis, your character exists on two entirely different planes of reality."

"Groovy."

"On the reality plane, as you noted, you're a drug dealer."

Hopper laughed nervously, his amusement bursting out of him like a wild steer at a rodeo.

"His name is Max," Roger continued. "He wants to bring out the Max in the people around him. You smoke a marijuana reefer and you provide the acid to Peter Fonda's guide, John. On the other plane, the plane of the trip, you play the character of the Judge. You put Peter on trial. Or rather, Peter puts himself on trial in a court where you preside." Roger gestured to where they were sitting.

Hopper's perceptions keened as he arrived at the deduction: "He wants to be groovy."

"Exactly," Roger grinned. "But he's not. How he gets there is his journey. Our story."

Hopper chuckled in an ornery way. "Oh, you're good, man!" He stood and took a more indulgent look at the set taking shape around them—the dumpy carousel, the gymnasium streamers, the head shop posters of Che, Dylan, and Chairman Mao. He snorted with amused derision. "My courtroom is looking a little like the Glendale High School prom, man."

"Only in the head of the Paul character," Roger grinned. "Who knows, he may have high school prom issues!"

"Okay, so the way you see it, Max is, like, both the outlaw *and* the law enforcer."

"I like that interpretation. You're Max, but you're also Peter's Super Ego, essentially."

"I dig that, man," Hopper approved. "Like I'm his fear. The thing that makes him straight, personified. Because he saw me in charge of a side of the world that's new to him, a level of being he fears and doesn't really understand. Far out."

"Heads up!" came a special effects man's voice from the far end of the soundstage. "Smoke test!"

A sudden, big whoosh then sounded, bouncing off the walls and high ceiling, followed by whorls of blue smoke spreading low to the ground.

Roger knew it would look just the right shade of cerulean in Pathécolor. As the undulating edge of the effusion came within their reach, Hopper bent over to stroke the billowing cloud like the back of a cat. It seemed to arch its spine in feline response.

"Jack? You wanted to see me?" The words came from a blur passing through the hectic corridors.

"If you have a minute," the loiterer managed, stepping out of his daze.

"I can give you two. Follow me, there's a place around here where we can sit down."

Roger guided Jack down and across the hall to a makeshift rest area containing a few well-cushioned chairs, a table with a radio, and a homey atmosphere. Roger took a seat, but Jack remained in the frame of the doorway, speaking conspiratorially and keeping an eye out for potential eavesdroppers.

"I have some very good casting news to report, Jack," Roger opened. "Susan Strasberg has agreed to play the part of Sally."

Jack's eyes doubled in size.

The daughter of Lee and Paula Strasberg, the flesh-and-blood sibling of Method acting itself?

"Isn't she kinda . . . overqualified?" he asked, sinking slowly into a chair.

"Possibly," Roger allowed, "but we'll take her. She's married to a young actor named Christopher Jones—they're calling him the new James Dean. They made a picture together, shot independently, and American International acquired it for distribution. Sam and Jim seized the opportunity to sign them both to three-picture contracts. So, it's a convenience for all concerned, and one that's very much to our advantage."

"Far out."

"What did you want to see me about, Jack?"

"I know things are gonna go before the camera soon, and it's just that . . . well, you haven't asked me for anything more. No notes, no rewrites, no nothin'. I guess I can't help worrying about it. I need to believe you're still on board with what I wrote."

Roger leaned forward. "Jack, we've been all through this! It's an astonishing piece of work, a boldly new conception—a totally new direction."

"That's kinda what I'm sayin'," Jack struggled to explain. "I want you to remember that—in this one—the Big Show happens up here." His eyebrows arched as he pointed to his temple.

If there was anything that Roger Corman disliked doing on a film set, it was doing the same job twice. Clearly, this project was deeply personal to Jack, and he needed to reassure him about it, once and for all, if he was ever going to have any peace. He beckoned Jack closer with a confidential flutter of his fingers. Jack took a quick look into the corridor and took the seat nearest Roger, who frankly had no idea of what he was about to say—but trusted himself in such situations.

"Jack, you're familiar with the underground film movement, right?"

"You mean Jonas Mekas, Maya Deren, Kenneth Anger—those kinda people?"

"Exactly. With *The Trip*, it's my goal to bring the underground film movement above-ground. Counter-cultural content. Rock music. Fractured continuity. Death to linear narrative."

Jack's expression brightened, then burned, with a glow that Roger could understand someone interpreting as demonic. So *that's* what Sandy saw during their LSD therapy!

"Roger," he said, looking sideways, "you could be blowin' smoke up my ass, or you might actually know what the hell you're doin'!"

Roger laughed good-heartedly. "Jack, look at it this way," he proposed. "If you keep writing scripts this good, you'll never have to work for me again!"

CHAPTER 14

FEBRUARY 1967

THE SPECIAL EFFECTS CREW unleashed some well-appointed poofs of carbon dioxide, turning the plain mid-day air into the sensuous haze of a dream state, then hustled ass out of the way.

"And... Action!" called Roger.

His cast and crew, a compact unit of approximately 15 people, were assembled outside the entrance of the cave at Bronson Caverns in Griffith Park. Aside from the mystic mists left to undulate here and there, the location was absolutely naked and true to life, looking much more like itself than it did on television as the entrance to the Batcave. A decade before the Batmobile had zoomed out of its egress, it was here where the Crab Monsters had staged their Attack, and where It Conquered the World—or tried to, both under Roger's direction when he was still a bit wet behind the ears.

This time it was a human consciousness occupying the cave. Stepping out, on cue, into the bold light of day was Peter Fonda, emerging from the cave dressed as a romantic hero in a white shirt with billowing sleeves. As TV commercial director-turned-acidhead Paul Groves, Peter's wardrobe approximated the fantasy wear Roger recalled from his own psychedelic experience.

Greeting him outside, on either side of the cave's maw, were two stuntwomen on horseback, wearing black hoods and cloaks. It had proved impossible to secure any black horses, similar to those Roger had seen in the midst of his trip, so a pair of piebald nags bore the indignity of being painted. Chicks in black capes, faces in shadow, it wasn't like anything Peter recollected from his own trips, but this wasn't about him, and he trusted the lead of his adventurous director. He was a Fonda, nothing if not a professional actor, and he saw it as his job—his purpose—to help his director express himself, even if this particular interlude had no parallel in Jack Nicholson's original script.

In separately filmed medium shots filmed about 15 minutes earlier, each woman had in turn removed her hood, revealing first the tumbling dark brown hair of Paul's ex-wife Sally (played by Susan Strasberg) and then the resplendent blonde hair of Paul's fantasy girl, Glenn. Glenn was played by Salli Sachse, a beautiful California actress and bikini model noted for her strong clavicle, which could make any bowman's heart leap. Salli had been one of AIP's most enduring contract players, mostly seen as background in the *Beach Party* pictures—smiling, dancing, clapping her hands, listening soulfully as Annette Funicello sang to her pillow at slumber parties. Salli's husband Peter, a promising young folk musician, had met his untimely death in an airplane crash in July and she had responded to the tragedy by throwing herself into her career; *The Trip* was her first step into the foreground, as it were. She made an extraordinary blonde, the hair color's effect multiplied when she donned a white pants suit and became a glorious tall vanilla milkshake of a woman, but it was not her natural color. She hated coloring it because it was a modest assault on the image she had spent years building up, but Susan Strasberg certainly wasn't about to go *shiksa* for this. Salli was loyal to AIP and bit the bullet for featured billing.

Peter wasn't looking at either Susan or Salli at this precise moment, but rather at the less lovely faces of two stuntwomen who, at Roger's signal, rode their galloping horses out of frame, their dark cloaks undulating in the breeze behind them—an action scripted to expose a path of strewn flower petals extending to the edge of the beach, a detail red-penciled as unnecessary expense as the day of filming drew near.

Also present in the shot were various friends of the production, mostly female, covered from head to foot in dense, clinging, black material with only their masks sheer enough to see through as they moved furtively around. They might be ghosts; they might be the shadows of the living in the wake of Paul's ego death; they might be the secret architects of waking consciousness; or they might simply be points of mystery and curiosity scattered within shots to enliven them. Roger didn't really know what they were or supposed to be but, one day, a little voice spake into his ear and he knew they had to be there.

Peter watched the two horsewomen goading their equines out of the shot and held an expression of awe and mystification, hoping that one of the two cameras on site would grab it.

"Cut... and Print!" Roger directed. "Ladies and gentlemen, we are now on the wrong set. The next shot is over that hill."

The film's assistant director Paul Rapp repeated Roger's instruction, but everyone was already mobilized and moving in the direction designated. Time was money and Roger's watch was ticking.

Frances made some quick notes on the scene and rose from her canvas chair. She was serving, as usual, as his personal assistant and script girl. Holding her production notebook, she walked over to where Roger was standing. Each time they worked together on a new film, it surprised her anew what a different man her boss was on the set. He was rigorously focused; the picture in his mind was the only thing in front of him, only the picture mattered. They were developing a form of working telepathy; he started talking to her almost before she arrived at his side.

"Frances, I know it's not in budget," he said, "and not even geographically accurate, but it's important to me that the reverse angle of this shot be the Keyhole Arch up at Big Sur."

"Right," she said, adding this information to her book.

"Find someone who can go up there with Peter and a camera and a roll of film and bring back the coverage we need. Not just the Keyhole Arch, but the whole area."

She consulted her book quickly. "He's needed on set every day this week... oh, and next. How shall we handle this?"

"Have a word with him. Ask if he would do it on a Sunday. If it doesn't work out, we'll have to add it in post, but I need that footage."

Roger's attention briefly turned to the surreal image of Angelo, his dwarf actor, sitting nearby on a rock, smoking a butt and looking at a racing form as he waited to film his scene. His wandering eye turned next to his cameraman Arch Dalzell, who had been with him on *The Little Shop of Horrors* and seemed to be holding court with his operator and a few others rather than getting his camera equipment to where it would soon be needed.

"*Gentlemen*," Roger addressed them firmly, "our next shot is over there." He didn't have to say it a third time.

Roger and Frances prepared to lead the procession to the next location as two or three shadow figures followed up the rear. As Roger marched on, he found himself eavesdropping on the *sotto voce* chatter behind them.

One of the shadows had pulled off her opaque headgear to get some fresh air. "Ah! I can breathe again! I could sure use a cigarette."

"You're not carrying them?"

"I left them in my bag back in the dressing area." A few moments passed in further marching, and then: "I wonder if there's time to run back there and grab one?"

"Ask Roger."

"I don't want to bother him. Not over a smoke. He's got a lot on his mind."

"He's actually a very nice man."

It was the cadence of these words that halted Roger's movements and made him turn around. He spoke without thinking: "Julie?"

The still-masked shadow figure removed her headgear, freeing a tumble of long auburn hair. It was indeed Julie Halloran.

"I didn't recognize you," he exclaimed, breaking into a grin.

"I would have unmasked myself earlier but you've been having a busy morning," she laughed.

"How did you . . . ?"

"Frances called and asked if I might come down and lend a hand."

Roger shot a look at Frances, who shrugged her shoulders as if to say, "Guilty."

"She did, did she? Well, this is a really nice surprise. We should continue walking. As for you," he addressed the other shadow figure, "you're not in the next shot, but you're in the one after that. You have ten minutes—go!"

She ran off in the direction of the dressing tents like an Olympian.

Roger, Julie, and Frances continued walking uphill.

Roger was the first to break the silence. "Julie, I'm . . . sorry I haven't been in touch. I've been busy with . . . well, with reaching this point."

"I understand. It's okay. It's exciting to be here."

"A lot of people find film sets boring," Frances offered.

"Oh, not me!" Julie said. "Everybody assembled with a common purpose, working toward a common goal. It's kind of like working in a newsroom, where everybody is working toward the next day's edition, but a lot more fun. Hey, is somebody having a problem over there?"

Julie had noticed that a couple of guys entrusted with moving a portion of the camera equipment were trying to do the work of three and having difficulties.

"They can't do all that *and* move a reflector," Roger pointed out. "Gentlemen," he called out in their direction, "find an extra pair of hands. We start shooting in five."

"Excuse me," Julie said, suddenly running toward them. "Can I help?"

That was in five.

In two, Roger was poised at the helm of the crew, his eyes narrowed and focused on the hillside crest where the last stragglers of the company were due to appear. His face broke into a sunny grin as Julie appeared, a shadow figure doing her best to carry a bulky reflector while engaged in a serious conversation with a guy on the camera crew, who was explaining to her the workings of the strange piece of equipment he was carrying. He watched with pleasure as he saw her pitching in, not only carrying the reflector down, but looking on with visible keenness as she paid close attention to how the crew took care to position it.

By the time the next shot was ready for filming, Julie had returned to Roger's side.

"Problem solved," she reported.

CHAPTER 15

July 1967

"WHAT'S THE BIG DEAL, Roger? It's just a private screening, not the fornicating Academy Awards!"

Sam Arkoff reached forward with a grunt, tapping a long but rock-solid accumulation of ash from his cigar into an ashtray on Roger's desk. The ashtray depicted an art deco arrangement of swank cars and spotlights behind a banner reading "Hollywood, California."

Roger, seated behind his desk, was covered in a barber's sheet as a Mexican hairdresser named Consuela freshened his haircut. It was one thing to have scissors snipping precariously around one's ears, but having to contend with Sam's arch, whiny voice at the same time made Roger feel all the more tense. That said, there are times in the oft-adversarial relationships between director and producer when opportunities to bond as part of the same team should be seized.

"I know, Sam," Roger said, "but this one's more important than the others."

"More important than *The House of Usher*? Than *Pit and the Pendulum*? From your mouth to the ear of the Pantages box office!"

"I want everything about it to be right. I want Peter and Jack to be proud of it. As proud as I am."

Every film shoot has its surprises, but this one had gone more or less according to plan. Roger, working with AIP's staff editor Ron Sinclair, had assembled a cut that he found quite pleasing within its budgetary limitations. He had fallen prey to some second thoughts here and there, which had obliged him to make certain concessions during the production; for example, he felt obliged to include some episodes of darkness in the trip sequence itself because he was aware that some people did have bad trips. This had annoyed Peter as well as Jack, but Roger truly believed that, once they saw the film, the final result would earn their respect. The extended special psychedelic effects sequences, that showed kaleidoscopic light shows pouring out of people's mouths and spreading across their faces, combined with some jazzy, arty second-unit material that Dennis and Peter had grabbed one Benzedrine-fueled night on the Sunset Strip, meant that *The Trip* would be smuggling into commercial theaters at least 20 full minutes of content that could legitimately be described as experimental or *avant-garde*. As Roger watched his cut straight through for the first time, he had re-experienced the sense of sensory bombardment he had felt during his own trip, as well as its sensuousness, its eroticism, and even its lunacy. He believed it was a good, fair, representational picture, despite certain acceptable compromises—then he sent the reels to Sam and Jim to prepare for release.

"Can you please sit more still, Mr. Corman?" asked Consuela. "No need to be nervous."

"Of course not!" Sam exclaimed, though in an exclamation that sounded like a jeer. "This guy's made 50 pictures and never lost a dime!"

"You know," Roger said, turning raconteur, "back at Stanford, I had to take this aptitude test and I scored 99 out of 100 on everything. It was weird."

As Roger reminisced to bolster his own good humor, Sam reached over and picked up a hand mirror from Consuela's arsenal of tools. He examined his own thinning hair. "Uh-huh. Very nice."

"Except accounting," Roger underlined, making his point. You know what my score was? Out of a hundred?"

"89?"

"Eleven. They said I could do whatever I wanted, but 'Stay away from numbers!'"

"Must be why you bat 'em so far out of the park, Rog. Say, Consuelo, you think you could do something to make my hair look like his?"

Consuela threw a glance up to God and kept snipping.

"Here I am, not *too* late!" said Frances from the doorway, holding a bucket of popcorn. "Hello, Sam."

"Hiya, gorgeous," purred the producer, reaching over for a fistful of corn. "When you gonna leave him and come work for me?"

She flashed a shallow smile, then turned to Roger. "Still feeling skittish?"

"Bearing up," he said as the sounds of snipping drew closer to his ears.

"Nothing says 'A Night at the Movies' like popcorn," Sam said, relieving Frances of the bucket while still chewing his first mouthful. "Roger, I want you to know that Jim and I are 100% united in our tremendous excitement about this picture."

"Thank you, Sam."

"The ads are lookin' good, our branch offices—New York, Boston, Cincinnati—they're all over the moon. 'Touch the scream that crawls up the wall!' Whatever the hell that means, but the test campaigns scored big. All signs are pointing to a bigger opening than we had for *The Wild Angels*—and we all know how well that did."

"Excellent."

"Of course, the lawyers suggested a couple of minor changes to cover our butts, but other than that . . . "

A sharp yelp came from the other side of the room. Consuela was cutting the hair behind Roger's ear when his head spun around toward Sam, unexpectedly.

"Did I cut you?"

Roger yanked off the sheet and jumped defensively to his feet.

"Just what did you do, Sam?"

"Minor changes. You won't even notice them!"

The office screening room, which seated maybe 30, was packed. Though the audience was compact in number, it nevertheless broke up into noticeable factions. Jim Nicholson was standing near the screen, trying to entertain Hilda Arkoff and his own wife; Bruce Dern was there with his wife, Dianne; Peter Fonda, Dennis Hopper and Jack Nicholson were there, all of them wearing shades at night; Peter Bogdanovich, Chuck Griffith and—a special invited guest—French critic Etienne Lipschitz grabbed whatever seats had not been claimed. Jim waved to get the attention of Roger and the others as they entered the room, having saved a row of seats off to the side for them.

The lights dimmed almost immediately as they took their seats. Frances, now aware of Roger's tension to the point of sharing it, reached into her purse and handed him a brace of Number 2 pencils.

"Don't bite your nails," she whispered. "Hold onto these."

Roger squeezed them tightly in expectation of the AIP fanfare, played as usual over an image of the United States Capitol building proudly domed against a beautifully clouded, blue sky. He looked over at Sam in the dark, sitting next to his Hilda—not this film's ideal audience, certainly—and became immediately aware of a knife poised against the throat of his child. Yes, somehow—against his own better judgment—Roger's own blood and brains and bowels had been invested in what his logical mind knew perfectly well was only a well-crafted piece of product, cranked out for a limited shelf life.

His cut had opened with a length of the kaleidoscopic effects work, flashing over the Electric Flag cue called "Peter's Trip," for which he had left explicit instructions about how the credits were to appear. Instead, the print being projected opened with a black screen, over which scrolling white text appeared.

You are about to be involved in a most unusual motion picture experience, intoned a narrator out of *Dragnet*. ***It deals fictionally with the hallucinogenic drug, LSD. Today, the extensive use in black market production of this and other such 'mind-bending' chemicals is of great concern to medical and civil authorities...***

Roger whispered tersely enough for everyone in the darkened room to hear him: "A *disclaimer*?"

Someone else in earshot muttered a miserable "fuck." It could have come from any number of people.

The illegal manufacture of these drugs is dangerous and can have fatal consequences...

Jim Nicholson, about six seats away, leaned forward and responded more quietly. "Roger. Think of the lawsuits. What if some kid sees this movie and takes a swan dive out a three-story window?"

Many have been hospitalized as a result.

"You want to disclaim your own movie?"

"All this scrolling, man," muttered Dennis Hopper. "Makes me feel like I'm going down in an elevator. Wow."

"Words," said Sam Arkoff blithely. "Just words."

"You know we're right, Roger," Jim reasoned. "Legally and, um, morally."

Brazenly, Etienne Lipschitz loudly shushed everyone. He was in church.

The picture represents a shocking commentary on a prevalent trend of our time and one that must be a great concern to all.

Roger snapped his first Number 2 pencil.

Seventy-some minutes later, the penultimate reel reached its end. In Roger's original cut, the non-sequitur images noted in Jack's original script—shots of the desert, reptiles striking and feeding, sun shining, tarantulas of thought being expressed in kaleidoscopes from the mouth—accelerated and gradually achieved the pitch of sensory bombardment he recalled from his trip, but his friends of AIP only saw excess and redundancy and whittled it down to a procession robbed of all meaning and intensity. The last of the film's five reels had now very nearly unraveled on the mounts of the rear projector. On the screen—after a night of sexual bliss and sensory ecstasy in Glenn's Malibu bedroom—Paul Groves awoke and found his way outside to greet the new day, the first day of his new awareness.

"It's easy now," said Glenn in voice-over. "Wait till tomorrow."

"I'll worry about that tomorrow," he replied, as the ticking music of The Electric Flag exploded in a sonic sunburst of pure nirvana.

Roger felt his heart surge forward. Something of the film he'd intended was still there. He could have almost forgiven the cuts Sam and Jim had inflicted on it—but then... at that exact moment in time, an optical—

slapped on in post-production—fractured Peter Fonda's final close-up with the sound of smashed glass.

Roger snapped two Number 2s at once. He glowered at Sam Arkoff.

"Whose brilliant idea was that?" he demanded.

"Rog, please," urged Jim Nicholson, "let's all calm down and take this conversation somewhere private."

"You want someplace private?" Roger jeered. "Pick any theater where you've booked this picture to open! Once word gets around, no audience this film was meant for will want to see it."

The end credits were brief, but followed by an extended Exit Music passage of plangent sitars and guitars and tablas, meant to keep audiences mellow, upbeat and expectant as they left the theater.

Instead of being unified by the experience, the audience for this private screening broke up into tribes. Peter Fonda and Roger exchanged disappointed looks, then the actor sauntered out, followed by a confused Dennis Hopper. On their way out, they passed Bruce Dern, munching trail mix and looking surprised. Outside, Peter and Dennis mounted their choppers, kicked heavy metal thunder into being, and steered off into the heart of the night.

Peter Bogdanovich watched the muted argument between Roger and his producers from a safe distance, seemingly aware that he was watching film history in the making. He hoped he would never end up disappointing Roger this way.

Frances withdrew quietly, offering in parting a sad little wave across the room to Jack, sunk in his seat, squirming a little as he forced a smile. Outside, she took a seat on the bench at the nearest bus stop, where Chuck Griffith joined her. They didn't say much to each other, though their thoughts of the adventures leading to this screening were much the same. Frances sighed a goodnight to Chuck as she caught the next blue bus home.

That night, after making herself some chamomile tea, she reached inside her bag and pulled out the notebook she had taken along to Big Sur last October. She had meant to share its scribbles with Roger in the wake of a successful evening, but things hadn't turned out as she had hoped. She smiled over the souvenir as she paged through it—watching legible sentences and words dissolving, sheet by sheet, into charming doodles and labyrinths and blossoming flowers.

Jack Nicholson was the next-to-last person to remain. A month or so earlier, Roger had kindly screened for him a rough cut of the picture. He had been impressed; it wasn't exactly his screenplay, of course—it would have been insane to expect so much—but it was a sincere effort and, without question, a higher level of Corman picture than he had ever seen. He'd felt good about it, even proud of it. He had been looking forward to seeing the finished version, all pretty and with the final music locked in, but what he'd just seen was like being blissed out at home when The Man suddenly breaks down your door for no better reason than the way you look and stomps all over your most precious things.

Sitting behind him, attentive and reverent until the last note of exit music shimmered into nothingness and the lights came up, was Etienne Lipschitz. The critic seized Jack's stunned hand in an enthusiastic vice of two.

"You should be proud!" he said, pumping it vigorously. "You have authored a masterpiece!"

He liked it, Jack thought numbly as he nodded without speaking. *My career's in the crapper and he likes it.*

Jack's career wasn't exactly in the crapper. Things were looking, if not exactly up, at least forward. He had recently finished *Hell's Angels on Wheels* and, come Sunday, he'd be flying up to San Francisco to start filming another hippie piece for AIP called *Psych Out*. At least this time it would be *him* up there on the screen humping Susan Strasberg.

He left the building, took a step off the curb onto the great winding way that was Sunset Blvd.—and stuck out his thumb.

As for Roger, he drove and drove until he stopped, and where he stopped was a short set of stairs that rose to a certain door, illuminated by a porch light. There were curtained windows, more softly lit, on either side. He got out of the car beneath the great exposure of a star-studded night sky. Despite the late hour, he pressed the doorbell. When it opened, he saw a dawning look of surprise that might as well have been his own, as he got his first real view of the next 50 years.

CHAPTER 16

Tick Tock

IN THE DAYS FOLLOWING THE screening, Roger dealt with his frustrations as best he could. As always, one of his favorite ways to unwind was on the tennis court. Jim Nicholson sometimes tagged along to provide him with a friendly opponent, or—if he happened to arrive alone—sometimes his club was able to provide a challenger. This was the case today, as Roger walked to the court he was assigned. He waited there, in his tennis whites, under a not-too-aggressive 1:30 p.m. sun.

Joining him was an older, silver-haired man of roughly his same height, his same weight, who also worked in the film business. They were well-matched in those respects, but Roger was initially concerned that this older gentleman mightn't be able to keep up with him. Roger was prepared to hold back, so the other man's powerful opening serve took him by surprise.

He quickly recalculated his defense and swung back with such ferocity, it looked like he wanted to destroy the ball rather than return it. It didn't matter. No matter what he put into his swing, the ball was always returned with equal—if not better—force. It proved a very competitive match.

They talked business. Roger held his racket at the ready, rocking back and forth on the soles of his tennis shoes.

"I think this was an example of the studio being just a little too afraid of the picture I made for them," he shouted across the net.

"I've been there," said the older man, measuring his serve. *Pow!*

"So," Roger shouted over the net, after socking the incoming ball with passion—*bam!* "They get their way, and we get screwed. That's what the story boils down to?"

"Not the whole story," grinned his counterpart, returning the ball. "It was just a chapter—part of the ending, but also the start of many beginnings."

"Name one." *Whack!*

"I'll do better than that. But first, think about this: *The Trip* became a huge hit."

Roger stopped, letting the ball bounce away.

"You're kidding."

"I'm not," the older man said, picking up a new ball. "When it came out that summer, *The Trip* grossed over six million dollars. Not a bad return on our investment."

He swatted the ball with precision, as if using it to illustrate his point. "Four hundred . . ." *Bam!* ". . . and fifty thousand!"

The older man returned his serve with a particularly artful play. This one got past Roger.

"Hey, nice move! Where'd you learn that?"

"You'll find out."

A look of understanding painted across Roger's face and he approached the net. The older man met him there, on the other side.

"You know, you look familiar," he told him.

"Not as familiar as you look to me," the older man smiled, sighing with nostalgia.

"Look, can you tell me something?"

"Only what you're ready to hear."

"I'm under contract to make two more pictures with Sam and Jim."

"Correct."

"What comes after that?"

"The realization that the only way to protect what you create is to sit in the chair where those decisions are made."

"You mean . . . I'll *become* Sam and Jim?"

"They're not bad guys. They were just doing what they felt was right for their company."

"They ruined my picture. That's right for their company?"

"Don't worry so much. The changes they made were just a moment in time. *The Trip* will outlast both of us, you'll see."

"But how? Cut to ribbons on *The Late Late Show*? Interrupted every ten minutes with commercials for beer and hemorrhoid cream?"

The other man showed a Cheshire-like smile as he peered into a future he had seen and approved.

"Let's just say you'll be pleasantly surprised."

Roger returned the older man's gaze, not quite knowing how to respond or how to take his answers. He would just have to follow through.

The two men returned to their playing positions. This time, Roger would deliver the opening serve. He took a ball, bounced it from the ground into his hand, and stood ready for the necessary energy to summon itself. However, he found himself distracted by an intrusive sound, a sound closer than the birds in the trees or the traffic passing by beyond the grounds. It was a ticking sound, the sound of time marching forward, the sound of things that needed to be done, things that only he could do.

"Time out," the other man called. He walked to the edge of the court, where he'd dropped his things, and carefully removed his wristwatch, leaving it there under a towel for safe-keeping.

Roger smiled indulgently. He was wearing his watch too, and wasn't about to take it off.

The older man, feeling lighter, jogged back into position on the court. He found his position and stood his ground with an expression that invited all.

Roger bounced the ball, gripped it, and spun his racket in a moment of peacockery.

His opponent chuckled; he'd been there.

"Hey," Roger shouted, "if you know so much, tell me this. *What is reality?*"

"Great question," smiled the older man. "*Let me think about it.*"

Roger's pensive expression gradually melted away, as the answer sunk in. He sized up his shot and belted the ball over the net into the next chapter.

EPILOGUE

THOUGH THE CONFLUENCE OF events that brought all of these friends and foes together for *The Trip* may have felt like a disaster at the time, it was anything but. It takes time for history to compile an honest accounting of itself, for perceived mistakes of the moment to be understood as genuine gifts to posterity.

Peter Bogdanovich used the opportunity Roger gave him, along with those two days of Boris Karloff's time, to make the first film he proudly signed with his own name: *Targets*. It was purchased for Paramount Pictures by producer Robert Evans for $150,000—putting it $20,000 into profit before it was ever released. When the film was released in August 1968, in the wake of the assassinations of Martin Luther King and Robert F. Kennedy, it was acclaimed by *The New York Times* as "a most auspicious feature debut for Bogdanovich . . . that scores an unnerving bullseye." It cleared the path for Bogdanovich to direct *The Last Picture Show*—a film that won him the Academy Awards for Best Director and Best Picture. He passed away on January 2, 2022 at the age of 82.

In September 1967, while in Toronto at a motion picture exhibitor's convention to help promote *The Trip* to overseas buyers, **Peter Fonda** was hiding out in his hotel room, getting high, when he found a still of himself in *The Wild Angels* that he had been asked to sign. Something clicked and he suddenly saw his biker image as the modern-day counterpart of the classic Western. He called **Dennis Hopper** and the two of them quickly concocted the central concept that became *Easy Rider*. They took the idea first to Roger Corman, hoping he would produce it for American International, but the deal fell through when Arkoff and Nicholson refused to fund the picture with Hopper as director. It was probably the worst decision Sam Arkoff would ever make. Made for a mere $40,000, *Easy Rider* ended up earning more than $60,000,000 in its initial release, making it the most successful independent film in motion picture history. After long and illustrious careers, Dennis died on May 29, 2010 (age 74); Peter died on August 16, 2019 (age 79).

Jack Nicholson got his divorce and continued hitch-hiking around Los Angeles for the next year or so. When **Bruce Dern** had to pass on the role written for him, Peter and Dennis rolled the dice and took a chance on Jack—casting him as the alcoholic Southern lawyer George Hanson in *Easy Rider*. No one anticipated what was going to happen during the filming; his performance is said to have sparked to life in the editing room. Ten years after his screen debut in *The Cry Baby Killer*, *Easy Rider* established Jack Nicholson as a major star "overnight"—at the age of 32. In years to come, both he and his buddy Derns would be recognized with the Academy Award for Best Actor. Many people consider Jack Nicholson to be the last of the classic Hollywood stars, and I don't disagree.

Frances Doel continued working as Roger's personal assistant until her retirement in 2017, during which time her mostly unsung duties extended to writing more than a dozen films—including the hugely successful *Big Bad Mama* (1974) and the genre-bending *Dinocroc* (2004). She has also produced five films, including the 1997 blockbuster *Starship Troopers*.

Charles B. "Chuck" Griffith likewise followed Roger to New World and continued to write scripts—including the highly successful *Death Race 2000*—and was eventually promoted to directing, as well. In 1982, Chuck's script for Roger's 1959 film *The Little Shop of Horrors* became a hit stage musical by Howard Ashman and Alan Menken. In the decades since, it was successfully filmed, and has become a perennial of live theater with productions mounted all over the world. He passed away in 2007, and I just want to say—in tribute—that his script for Roger's goofy monster satire *Creature from the Haunted Sea* (1961) is probably the closest thing the world had to a Thomas Pynchon story until Thomas Pynchon himself came along.

When American International went public in 1969, taking on a board of conservative shareholders, **Roger Corman** saw the writing on the wall. The creative clampdown he had been experiencing at the company was only going to get worse. After *The Trip*, Roger made two more movies for AIP: *Bloody Mama* and *Gas-s-s-s!* Sam and Jim tampered with both of them.

In 1970, after the box office success of *Bloody Mama*—a retelling of the Ma Barker story starring Shelley Winters and a young Robert de Niro—Roger asked his friend **Julie Halloran** if she might use her resources to research other female criminals of the Depression era. The story she recovered became *Boxcar Bertha*, her first production credit. It was the first Hollywood feature to be directed by Martin Scorsese and Roger's final production for AIP. Julie remembers: "After years of friendship, Roger and I suddenly found ourselves walking side by side, and we just kept on walking."

In May 1970, Roger settled into the chair where all his future decisions would be made—by forming his and Julie's own production and distribution company: New World Pictures.

On December 26 of that same year, **Roger and Julie** married, a union that went on to produce and distribute four children.

After 15 successful years, they sold the name "New World Pictures" as well as the going concern, and started anew under the banner of Concorde-New Horizons (now New Horizons Pictures).

In a job she was somehow doing before she realized she was doing it, **Julie Corman** has produced more than 35 feature films, working with such directorial luminaries as Jonathan Demme, John Sayles, Lewis Teague, and Adam Simon. At the turn of the century, she became Chair of NYU's Graduate Film School. She continues to produce.

During his first decade as a producer and director, Roger Corman had discovered and provided early opportunities to direct such promising talents as Francis Ford Coppola, Martin Scorsese, Peter Bogdanovich, Monte Hellman, Dennis Hopper, Curtis Harrington, Jack Hill, Daniel Haller, and Stephanie Rothman. In the five decades since the start of New World Pictures, he has produced or executive produced more than 300 films, while additionally fostering the careers of directors Jonathan Demme, Joe Dante, James Cameron, Ron Howard, John Sayles, Allan Arkush, Paul Bartel, producer Gale Ann Hurd, and numerous other Hollywood success stories, while also distributing important films by Federico Fellini, François Truffaut, and Akira Kurosawa. In 2009, he was presented with an Honorary Academy Award "for his rich engendering of films and filmmakers."

He continues to produce and his unmatched legacy continues to evolve in ways even he could not have foreseen.

To wit: In 2011, ***The Trip*** made its high-definition debut on the MGM HD cable channel. Though unannounced as such, this late-night broadcast quietly marked the first time Roger Corman's original, uncensored cut was made available to the general public. This version has since replaced in circulation the expurgated AIP cut, which prevailed for more than half a century.

Which just goes to show... Business may gain the upper hand in the short term—but in the long run, it's art that endures.

"No novocaine. It dulls the senses."

Charles B. Griffith,
The Little Shop of Horrors (1960)

WORKS CONSULTED

IN ADDITION TO PERSONAL INTERVIEWS, correspondence and conversations I have had over the years with **Roger Corman**, **Julie Corman**, **Frances Doel**, and **Samuel Z. Arkoff**, the information baked into this novel is the product of a lifetime of fascination with the 1960s—its films, its art, its music, its tensions and relaxations. The following references were especially useful in terms of providing me with relevant insights, personal trivia, and inspiration for various scenes.

Arkoff, Samuel Z. with Richard Trumbo. *Flying Through Hollywood by the Seat of My Pants* (New York, NY: Birch Lane Press, 1992).

Biskind, Peter. *Easy Riders, Raging Bulls* (New York, NY: Simon & Schuster, 1998).

Nasr, Constantin (editor). *Roger Corman: Interviews* (Jackson, MS: University Press of Mississippi, 2011).

Corman, Roger with Jim Jerome. *How I Made a Hundred Movies in Hollywood and Never Lost a Dime* (New York, NY: Renaissance/Random House, 1990).

Fonda, Peter. *Don't Tell Dad: A Memoir* (New York, NY: Hyperion Press, 1999).

Gray, Beverly. *Roger Corman: An Unauthorized Biography of the Godfather of Indie Filmmaking* (New York, NY: Renaissance Books, 2000).

McGilligan, Patrick. *Jack's Life: A Biography of Jack Nicholson* (New York, NY: W.W. Norton & Co., 2015).

McGee, Mark Thomas. *Faster and Furiouser: The Revised and Fattened Fable of American International Pictures* (Jefferson, NC: McFarland & Company, 1995).

McGee, Mark Thomas. *Roger Corman: The Best of the Cheap Acts* (Jefferson, NC: McFarland & Company, 1988).

Playboy Interview: Peter Fonda/Joan Baez (Chicago, IL: Playboy Press, 1971).

Silver, Alain and James Ursini. *Roger Corman: Metaphysics on a Shoestring* (Los Angeles, CA: Silman-James Press, 2006).

Carson, Greg. "Tune In, Trip Out." A DVD documentary featurette (17:16) included in MGM Home Video's DVD box set *The Roger Corman Collection* (2003). Also included with MGM's "Midnite Movies" double feature DVD of *Psych-Out* and *The Trip* (2014) and Signal One's UK Blu-ray of *The Trip* (2016).

Williams, Esther with Digby Diehl. *The Million Dollar Mermaid* (New York, NY: Simon & Schuster, 1999).

Page 48 quote from the song "I Had Too Much To Dream (Last Night)" by the Electric Prunes, written by Nancie Mantz and Annette Tucker, published by Sony/ATV ACUFF ROSE MUSIC / BMI.

ABOUT THE AUTHOR

TIM LUCAS IS NOW IN his 50th year as a published writer.

He is the author of the acclaimed alt-horror novel *Throat Sprockets* (1994) and *The Book of Renfield: A Gospel of Dracula* (2005), the mammoth critical biography *Mario Bava: All the Colors of the Dark* (2007), and monographs on the films *Videodrome* (2008) and *Spirits of the Dead/Histoires Extraordinaires* (2018). His novella *The Secret Life of Love Songs*, packaged with an original soundtrack of songs co-written with Dorothy Moskowitz, was released by PS Publishing in 2021.

The former publisher/editor of the long-running cult film review *Video Watchdog* (1990-2017), he has recorded nearly 150 audio commentaries for Blu-ray and DVD discs, including several for the films of Roger Corman. In 2011, he interviewed Corman over two nights before sold-out audiences at the St. Louis Film Festival's "Vincentennial" celebration.

In October 2016, his original screenplay *The Man with Kaleidoscope Eyes* (co-written with Charlie Largent, Michael Almereyda and James Robison) was presented as a live table reading at the Vista Theater in Los Angeles, narrated by director Joe Dante and starring Bill Hader as Corman, Roger Corman himself as the Real Roger, and Ethan Embry as Jack Nicholson. The theater heralded the performance as "The Greatest Movie Never Made!" and it received a standing ovation from its audience, which included Julie Corman, Peter Bogdanovich, and Jonathan Demme.

Tim is also the recipient of numerous awards, including two Saturn Awards (one for Special Achievement) and 20 Rondo Hatton Classic Horror Film Awards.